AUG 1 6 2022  P9-DTA-637

Danger at the Iron Dragon

NAPA COUNTY LIBRARY
580 COOMBS STREET
NAPA, CA 94559

Read all the mysteries in the

NANCY DREW DIARIES

NANCY Drew DIARIES™

Danger at the Iron Dragon

#21

CAROLYN KEENE

Aladdin

NEW YORK LONDON TORONTO SYDNEY NEW DELHI

If you purchased this book without a cover, you should be aware that this book is stolen property. It was reported as "unsold and destroyed" to the publisher, and neither the author nor the publisher has received any payment for this "stripped book."

This book is a work of fiction. Any references to historical events, real people, or real places are used fictitiously. Other names, characters, places, and events are products of the author's imagination, and any resemblance to actual events or places or persons, living or dead, is entirely coincidental.

ALADDIN

An imprint of Simon & Schuster Children's Publishing Division

1230 Avenue of the Americas, New York, New York 10020

First Aladdin paperback edition January 2021

Text copyright © 2021 by Simon & Schuster, Inc.

Cover illustration copyright © 2021 by Erin McGuire

Also available in an Aladdin hardcover edition.

All rights reserved, including the right of reproduction in whole or in part in any form.

ALADDIN and related logo are registered trademarks of Simon & Schuster, Inc.

NANCY DREW, NANCY DREW DIARIES, and related logo are trademarks of Simon & Schuster, Inc.

For information about special discounts for bulk purchases, please contact Simon & Schuster Special Sales at 1-866-506-1949 or business@simonandschuster.com.

The Simon & Schuster Speakers Bureau can bring authors to your live event. For more information or to book an event contact the Simon & Schuster Speakers Bureau at 1-866-248-3049 or visit our website at www.simonspeakers.com.

Series designed by Karin Paprocki

Cover designed by Heather Palisi

Interior designed by Mike Rosamilia

The text of this book was set in Adobe Caslon Pro.

Manufactured in the United States of America 1220 OFF

2 4 6 8 10 9 7 5 3 1

Library of Congress Cataloging-in-Publication Data

Names: Keene, Carolyn, author.

Title: Danger at the Iron Dragon / by Carolyn Keene.

Description: First Aladdin paperback edition. | New York : Aladdin, 2021. |
Series: Nancy Drew diaries ; #21 | Audience: Ages 8-12. | Summary: Nancy, Bess, and George's Jiu-Jitsu class at Iron Dragon MMA takes a dark turn when they discover a threatening message at the front desk, leading Nancy to investigate whether a rival academy is to blame.

Identifiers: LCCN 2020029215 (print) | LCCN 2020029216 (ebook) |
ISBN 9781534442030 (paperback) | ISBN 9781534442047 (hardcover) | ISBN 9781534442054 (ebook)

Subjects: CYAC: Mystery and detective stories. | Jiu-jitsu—Fiction.

Classification: LCC PZ7.K23 Daqm 2021 (print) | LCC PZ7.K23 (ebook) | DDC [Fic]—dc23

LC record available at https://lccn.loc.gov/2020029215

LC ebook record available at https://lccn.loc.gov/2020029216

Contents

Dear Diary,

I STARTED VOLUNTEERING DOWNTOWN at the soup kitchen a few weeks ago, and it's been going really well! It took a little while to learn how everything works and get into the swing of things, but now I think I'm getting the hang of it. I know that I've helped a lot of people over the years, solving mysteries and catching criminals, but giving back has always had a special place in my heart. It's great to get involved in the community and try new things. After all, you never know who you'll meet, or where you'll end up. . . .

CHAPTER ONE

Enter the Iron Dragon

"THAT'S IT FOR TONIGHT, NANCY!" CHEF Kathy called out, waving goodbye to our last customer and locking the front door. "Time to clean this place up."

I set down my ladle and breathed a sigh of relief. I loved volunteering at the River Heights Soup Kitchen, but standing at the counter and serving dinner to two hundred people was not an easy job. My feet were throbbing, my ladling arm was sore, and I could barely keep my eyes open. I hauled the now-empty stock-pot over to the big, industrial sink and helped Chef

Kathy, the kitchen manager, wash the dishes and get everything ready for the next meal in the morning. Kathy was a petite woman—with sparkling eyes and black hair hidden under a hairnet—but she carried vats of food and heavy boxes of supplies around with a strength that defied her small size. "I don't know how you do this every day," I said, awed. "I only work once a week, and I'm exhausted!"

Kathy, her hands full of suds, shrugged. "You do the impossible often enough, it becomes routine, I guess."

By the time Kathy and I were finished, it was almost eleven p.m. I peeled off my rubber gloves and hung my apron on a hook by the kitchen door. "See you next week?" I called out, slipping into my jacket and slinging my backpack over my shoulder.

"Yep, I'll be here," Kathy replied. "Thanks so much for your help, Nancy. And tell your dad I said hello!"

With a nod and a wave, I stepped out onto the street and turned my collar up against the cool night air. The soup kitchen was in an older section of downtown

River Heights, where many shop fronts sat empty and burned-out streetlamps rarely got replaced. There was a campaign going to help fix up this part of the city and get more help to the people who lived there. Dad was helping to organize it—that was how I became interested in volunteering at the soup kitchen in the first place. River Heights was my home, and I always tried to do what I could to make it better for everyone.

The street outside the soup kitchen was deserted, and only a few pools of light illuminated the sidewalk in front of me as I walked to my car. A slender crescent moon hung in the sky, dark clouds churning past it, reminding me just how late it was. I yawned, fighting to keep my eyes open. All I could think about was getting home to the warm comfort of my bed. I just wanted to sleep.

And then—a sound broke the silence.

Footsteps. Behind me, and approaching fast.

A bolt of adrenaline shot through me and I was instantly wide awake. Reaching into my pocket for my phone, I turned to face whoever was coming—but I was too late. A figure in dark, nondescript clothes was already on me, grabbing me by the arm and knocking the phone from my hand. In slow motion, I watched it skitter across the pavement out of arm's reach, right before I was slammed against a wall. I shouted out in pain as my face bounced against the brickwork, making my vision blur.

The mugger tried to pull off my backpack, but it was tangled around my arms and wouldn't come loose. I tried to focus my mind and figure out what to do, but I was dizzy and disoriented. "Don't do this," I managed to groan. "You don't need to do this."

"Just be quiet and let go of the bag," the mugger muttered.

"Look, if you need something, maybe I can—"

The mugger shook me violently, making the world spin. "I said, *be quiet!*"

And then—

"*Hey!*" someone shouted from down the street. "What do you think you're doing? Get off her!"

The tight grip on my shoulder loosened slightly

as the mugger froze. I turned to see a stocky young woman running toward us, moving in and out of the light cast by the streetlamps. She stopped just a few feet away from us and raised both hands to the sky. "Look, man," she said. "I don't want any trouble. Just let her go. Okay?"

The mugger's grip on me tightened once again. "If you didn't want any trouble, *little lady*," he sneered, his voice low and dangerous, "you came to the wrong place."

Swinging me by the handle of my backpack, the mugger threw me to the ground. I gasped with the impact and struggled to a sitting position against the wall. Fighting to stay conscious, I watched as the mugger advanced on the young woman, cracking his knuckles. He was easily a foot taller and fifty pounds heavier than she was. I could now see she had tawny brown skin and a halo of black curls poking out of the hoodie she was wearing. She dropped into a low, wide stance, her hands in front of her face.

The mugger chuckled. "What's all that, eh? You know karate or something?"

"Not exactly," the young woman said. A moment later she shot forward, slamming into the mugger like a freight train. In one smooth movement, she took his knees out from under him. He toppled over with a grunt of surprise.

He wasn't the only one. I was pretty surprised myself.

"You're really going to get it now, you little—" he started to say as he pushed himself up, fire in his eyes. But before he could even finish his sentence, the young woman had clambered onto his back and laced her arms and legs around his body like a human backpack. He struggled to stand, clawing at her hands and feet as he tried to wriggle free. The girl wrapped one of her arms under his chin, braced her other arm against the back of his head, and started to squeeze. I watched as after just a few seconds, the mugger's eyes fluttered closed and his entire body went limp. He collapsed into a heap, snoring.

After a moment, the young woman stood up and dusted off her jeans. She leaned down to pick up my phone from the ground and walked over, holding it out to me as I got to my feet slowly. My head was still spinning. It didn't even look like she'd broken a sweat.

"Here you go," she said pleasantly. "Are you okay?"

Maybe it was the head injury, or maybe it was the shock of witnessing this girl completely wreck a man twice her size, but instead of, *Yes, I'm fine* or *Thank you so much for saving my life*, I said, "Who are you, and how in the world did you do that?"

The young woman smiled, her brown eyes twinkling. I was amazed at how someone could look so tough and intimidating one minute, and so sweet and friendly the next. "Double leg takedown followed by a back take, and a rear naked choke for the finish," she said, matter-of-factly. "Nothing you couldn't manage with a little practice."

"Me?" I said.

"Sure, why not?"

I opened my mouth to answer, but nothing came out.

"Oh, uh, while you're thinking about it," the young

woman said, nodding at the phone in my hand, "you should probably call the police to come arrest this punk before he wakes up."

"Right," I said, unlocking my phone and dialing the number. "The police."

"I'm Carly, by the way. Carly Griffith."

I reached out to shake her hand. "Nancy Drew," I said with a grin. "You wouldn't believe how glad I am to meet you."

About half an hour later, after giving my statement to the police, I was sitting in the back of an ambulance, being monitored by the paramedics. With an ice pack pressed to my forehead, I watched as the mugger was read his rights and shoved into a squad car.

"That girl was definitely wearing brass knuckles or something!" I heard him saying. "She attacked *me*! She's dangerous!"

"Yeah, yeah," the police officer said, slamming the car door shut. "Whatever you say, buddy."

As the police car drove away, Carly walked up to

me. "Not used to being beaten up by a girl, I guess," she said with a shrug.

"You were amazing," I said. "Where did you learn to fight like that?"

Instead of replying, Carly turned around so I could see the logo on the back of her hoodie. It depicted a silvery white dragon head, its mouth open in a roar, with the words IRON DRAGON MMA encircling it. "It's a mixed martial arts academy a few blocks from here," she explained. "That's actually where I was coming from when I heard you cry out. There's a twenty-four-hour takeout place around the corner that I sometimes like to go to after class. Anyway, I've been training in Brazilian Jiu-Jitsu at Iron Dragon for about six months now. Before that I was at other schools for years."

"Brazilian Jiu-Jitsu?" I asked. "What's that? I've heard of karate and kung fu and tae kwon do before, but that one's new to me."

Carly blew out her cheeks. "Wow," she said after a moment. "That's a tough question to answer. There's no striking in Jiu-Jitsu, like in those other martial arts you mentioned. It's kind of a combination of wrestling and judo, which involves being able to throw your opponent to the ground and maintain a dominant position. But Jiu-Jitsu's more than that. It's self-defense, but it's also a sport. Kind of like chess, but with people. Really, it's a whole way of life. . . ." Carly must have noticed the confused expression on my face. She chuckled. "I sound crazy, don't I?"

"'Crazy' is a strong word," I replied. "'Passionate' is more what I was thinking."

"Honestly, it would be easier to just show you than try to explain it," she said.

"Show me?" I asked. "Oh, I don't know—" I shook my head, then winced as a wave of dizziness crashed over me.

"Hey," Carly said, putting a steadying hand on my shoulder. "You sure you're all right?"

"Yeah," I said, leaning back against the ambulance door until the dizziness faded. "The paramedics said it's just some bumps and bruises. I should be as good as new after a solid night of sleep."

"Oh, perfect!" Carly said, her face lighting up. "Then you'll be all set for tomorrow night's class."

I blinked. "Excuse me, what?"

"Jiu-Jitsu class at Iron Dragon," she said. "Eight o'clock to ten thirty. Our coach is great. You'll be fine!"

"I—but—" I stammered.

"Trust me," Carly said, as she started to back away. "Just give it a try! Bring a friend. Bring two! Once you train with us, muggers will think twice before coming after you again!"

Before I could protest any more, Carly had waved goodbye and disappeared into the night.

I pulled into our driveway a little while later, after the paramedics had cleared me to drive. Every part of my body was aching, and my mind had gone numb. I could hardly believe that it was still the same night that I'd spent ladling out chicken noodle soup!

I staggered to the front door, my bag dragging behind me, but it swung open before I could even reach for the knob. My father stood silhouetted in the doorway, dressed in his navy-blue bathrobe, which matched the dark circles under his eyes. "Nancy," he said, a mixture of anger, worry, and exhaustion coloring his voice. "Where *were* you?"

Seeing Dad like that blew the cobwebs from my brain. I realized that he had been expecting me home almost two hours before. In all the chaos of the mugging and the aftermath, I had completely forgotten to call. Plus, I'd turned my ringer off at the soup kitchen and never thought to turn it back on. "I'm—I'm so sorry," I said.

"I called you over and over again, and you didn't pick up," he said, his voice rising. "Then I called Kathy on her cell around twelve thirty, and she said you'd left at eleven. I was about to call the police when I saw your car coming up the street. Do you have *any* idea how worried I was? How could you—?"

As I stepped closer, into the light, Dad's face went pale. He reached out to touch the side of my head that had hit the brick wall, and I winced. Between my battered face, ripped jeans, and dirty jacket, I must have looked like a mess. "Honey," he whispered. "What happened?"

"I was walking to my car and this guy came out of nowhere," I began as Dad gently wrapped an arm around my shoulder and guided me into the welcoming warmth of the house. While he brewed us mugs of herbal tea in the kitchen, I sat at the table and told him the whole story: the attack, Carly's appearance, talking to the police, and something miraculous called "Brazilian Jiu-Jitsu."

"Well," Dad said, taking a sip of his tea, "you had quite a night."

"Yeah . . . I did. I really am sorry I didn't call. I don't know how I could have forgotten. . . ."

Dad laid a hand on my back and gave it a reassuring rub. "It's totally understandable. You were in shock. I see it all the time in witness statements after run-ins like this. People can't always think straight right after a traumatic event. I'm just glad you're okay. And I'm also glad Hannah is away visiting her sister this week and not here at the house. If you think I was worried, she would have been climbing the walls!"

Hannah Gruen, our housekeeper, *was* a bit of a mother hen. "Yeah," I said sheepishly. "You're not going to call her, are you?"

He shook his head. "No, she'd just come running back here to make a lot of soup and force you to stay in bed. Not that I don't enjoy her soup . . . but that woman needs a break! I'll let Hannah enjoy her vacation and tell her about your exploits when she gets back." With a chuckle, he added, "You'd think I'd be used to this kind of thing, what with my daughter being the preeminent amateur sleuth of River Heights. But even after all this time . . . I still worry about you, kid."

I smiled, a blush rising in my cheeks. "I know, Dad. But I really wasn't looking for trouble this time. I should have been paying more attention walking alone like that, but it happened so fast. . . . I was really lucky that Carly showed up when she did."

Dad sighed and leveled a serious look at me. "You sure were. But you might not be so lucky next time, which is why I think you should take that young woman up on her offer."

"What?" I sputtered. "You mean you want me to learn Jiu-Jitsu?"

Dad nodded. "Absolutely. Honestly, I can't believe we've gone this long without you learning some kind of self-defense. If you're going to continue taking on cases and dealing with criminals, you've got to know how to protect yourself. This is the perfect opportunity to do just that."

I bit my lip. Without a doubt, Dad was right. I loved being an amateur detective, but it wasn't the safest job in the world. There'd been plenty of times that I'd faced off against dangerous people, with no real idea of how to defend myself, but I'd never actually considered learning a martial art. I wasn't particularly athletic, either—I mean, sure, I played a little soccer and softball in school, but I had a feeling that one-on-one combat would be a whole different ball game.

Dad placed his palms on the counter and leaned in close. "Look, what's the worst that could happen?

You decide it's not your cup of tea, you walk away with a little bit of new knowledge and experience. If you don't try it, you'll never know. And anyway, I think there are two girls you could probably convince to go along with you. . . ."

I sighed and rubbed my eyes with the backs of my hands. "You think you're pretty smart, don't you, Dad?"

He grinned. "I mean, I *am* your father. You do get it from somewhere."

I couldn't help but smile back. "Oh, *all right*," I finally said. "I'll do it."

Dad clapped his hands. "Good girl. You've made your old man very happy. Now, let's get some sleep. Tomorrow, your training begins."

CHAPTER TWO

~

Fight Night

IN THE EIGHTEEN HOURS BETWEEN MY head hitting the pillow and me driving to Iron Dragon MMA, I had managed to convince myself that this whole Jiu-Jitsu thing was a good idea. Like Dad had said, it would be good to learn some self-defense, especially in my line of work. Plus, it was just one class—it couldn't hurt to give it a try.

It wasn't until I parked in front of the academy and saw two guys roughly the size of pickup trucks walking in that I considered that maybe—just maybe—this was actually a very, *very* bad idea.

But since I'd convinced my best friends Bess Marvin and George Fayne to tag along, I had to at least pretend to be excited. Bess was sitting next to me in the front seat, looking like a bundle of nerves, while George sat in the back, doing vigorous neck and shoulder stretches. "Well," I said brightly, pulling my key out of the ignition. "This should be fun!"

"It's all fun and games until someone hits you in the face," Bess said darkly. She had taken significantly more convincing than George.

"Actually," George broke in, "it's highly unlikely you'd get hit in the face in Jiu-Jitsu. The submission techniques are mostly chokes and joint locks. I did a little online research this afternoon—"

"Of course you did," I muttered with a grin.

"Chokes? Joint locks?" Bess turned to me. "Nancy, what have you gotten us into? Isn't it enough that we're regularly running into—and away from—danger? Now we're just going to start paying people to break our arms?"

I shrugged. "What can I say? My dad made me do it."

Bess sighed and lugged her gym bag out of the car. "After tonight—if we survive this—I'll have to have a word with Mr. Drew. . . ."

Not really knowing what to expect, the three of us came wearing whatever workout clothes we had on hand. Bess was in pastel yoga pants and a stretchy tank top, her blond hair gathered into a neat bun. George wore black leggings and a gray muscle shirt that had the words ALWAYS HUNGRY printed on the front. Her short, dark hair was messy and windblown as always— I doubted she even owned a hairbrush at this point. It drove Bess crazy, but personally, I always liked George's carefree look. As for me, all I really had was my running gear—electric-blue leggings and a short-sleeved white workout top. I'd tied my strawberry-blond hair back into a simple ponytail and was hoping for the best.

The academy was in a long, low building next to a branch of the Heights Bank. There were a corner store and a gas station nearby, but other than that, the street was mostly homes and empty, boarded-up shops with FOR SALE signs posted out front.

After glancing in nervously through the plate-glass window, I pushed through the front door and stepped into a lobby. The room was furnished with a wide gray desk, and the wall behind it was adorned with the same dragon logo that I'd seen on the back of Carly's hoodie. There was a shelf overflowing with trophies and medals nearby, and a framed newspaper article from the *River Heights Bugle* on the wall. It was all about the academy and featured a picture of a serious-looking man with black hair and glasses, and what looked like a team photo. Beyond that, a handful of students chatted together in a sitting area with a sofa and chairs.

A girl with long blond hair and a big smile rose from her seat behind the desk to greet us. "Hi there!" she said cheerfully. "Welcome to Iron Dragon MMA! My name is Libby. How can I help you ladies?"

I opened my mouth to reply, but George beat me to it. "We are here to fight!" she said. A little bloodthirsty for my taste, but that's George for you.

Bess rolled her eyes.

"We'd like to try out one of your classes," I

explained. "One of your students invited us to—"

"Nancy? I thought that was you!" I turned to see Carly, dressed in a white uniform with a purple belt tied around her waist, jogging up to us. "You actually came!" she said, delight spreading across her face. "And you brought friends! Two of them!"

I smiled. "Well, you did tell me to."

"I know, but that doesn't always work. Actually, it almost never works." She clapped her hands in excitement. "I'm so happy you guys are here!"

Within minutes, Libby had picked out a rental uniform—traditionally called a "gi"—for each of us and given us each a white belt to wear. "We have Jiu-Jitsu classes from eight to ten thirty on Mondays, Tuesdays, and Thursdays, and some morning classes on the weekend," Libby told us. "We're closed on Wednesdays and Fridays, but we often have people come in for private lessons on those days, if you're interested."

"Let's see if we survive first," Bess said, and we followed Libby to the women's locker room.

After pulling the stiff, rough jacket and pants on

over my workout clothes and figuring out how to tie the belt, the three of us walked to the training area, where all the other students were gathering. It was a large, industrial-looking space with a high ceiling and wall-to-wall black and gray mats covering the floor like a giant checkerboard. "Nancy, Bess, George—let me introduce you to some of the regulars!" The other students turned toward us, curious. "That's Jake, Ernesto, Jamie, Tim, Penny, Ryan—don't roll with him, he's crazy—Erica—"

"Hey!" Ryan protested.

"Nate, Liam," Carly continued, not missing a beat. "And that's Jeremy."

"Hello," said Jeremy, a tall, broad-shouldered young man with deep brown skin and glasses, who was wearing a blue belt. He gave me a friendly slap on the back that almost sent me flying.

"FYI, Jeremy is bigger than he looks," Carly murmured under her breath.

"He looks pretty big, though," I murmured back.

"Ah, yep."

Jiu-Jitsu, line it up!

~ 22 ~

I turned to see a man standing at the front of the room, hands on hips, waiting expectantly. His salt-and-pepper hair and beard were cropped close, and he was probably at least six inches shorter and fifty pounds lighter than Jeremy and some of the other big guys in the room. But between the look on his face and the black belt circling his waist, I could tell that this was not a man to be taken lightly.

"Who's that?" I asked Carly.

"Ethan Sekula, head coach," she said, herding me and my friends toward the mats. "C'mon, let's go. No time to chat now!"

"But what do we do?" said George.

"Just do what everyone else does," Carly replied.

With military precision, all the students lined up by belt color—brown belts at the front, then purple belts, blue belts, and white at the rear. I stood next to the girl named Penny, nervously shifting my weight from one foot to the other. She was about my height, with wavy brown hair and a heart-shaped face. Penny was humming under her breath, and after a moment I realized it was "Take Me Out to the Ball Game." When she noticed me watching her, she gave me an encouraging smile.

"I thought we were here to fight," I joked. "Not play baseball."

Penny chuckled. "I can't help it. I used to play when I was a kid, and the song stuck with me ever since. First class?"

I nodded.

"Nervous?"

I blushed. "Is it that obvious?"

"Looks like we've got some new people in tonight," Coach Ethan said, and I jerked back to attention when I realized he was looking straight at me. I waved awkwardly. "Just don't break them, please," he told the class. "Ideally, we'd like them to come back."

I glanced over to Bess, whose pale face was now tinged with green. *Help me,* she mouthed.

George, meanwhile, looked like she was about to ride a roller coaster. "This is so cool!" she whispered.

"Bow in," Coach Ethan commanded. After we all did, he said, "Start jogging!"

After a ten-minute routine that had me panting and dripping with sweat, Coach Ethan signaled that we could take a water break. We regrouped in a semi-circle and sat down on the mats. "Okay, guys! Good warm-up," he said, clapping his hands.

"That was the *warm-up*?!" asked George. She looked like she'd run a marathon.

"Today we're going to go over the basic hip toss," Coach Ethan continued. "Ryan, come out."

Ryan, a lanky blue belt who looked to be about my age, hopped up from the floor and stood in front of the coach. "So, we get our normal collar and sleeve grips on the gi, step and turn in, load them up onto our back, and extend the arm to complete the throw," Coach Ethan explained. With one fluid movement, he lunged at Ryan and launched him over his back and onto the mat with a thud.

I winced, expecting to see Ryan writhing on the ground, in pain or unconscious. Miraculously, he jumped back up like nothing had happened and stood at the ready for another.

"Whoa," Bess murmured.

The coach did the move twice more, explaining different details each time. "Got it?" he asked, scanning the room. His gaze stopped on me. "New girl!" he said, pointing a finger in my direction. "What's your name?"

"Nancy Drew," I answered.

"What's with the deer-in-the-headlights look, Nancy Drew?"

I blinked. "Well, I mean, it's my first day, and I don't really understand how—"

Coach Ethan lowered his chin and looked down his nose at me. "Come out," he ordered.

It was my turn to feel a little queasy. Steadying my breath, I stepped into the center of the circle. "Get your grips," he said, before walking me through the rest of the setup.

"Now, throw me," he said.

"But you're bigger than I am," I said hesitantly. "How am I supposed to—?"

"Don't think about it, just do it!" he said firmly.

Swallowing hard, I closed my eyes and calmed my mind. *Just do it,* I repeated to myself. When I opened my eyes again, I grabbed his collar and sleeve, twirled around, and threw a full-grown man over my shoulder and onto the ground.

Bam! His body hit the mat with another thud. A second later, he was back up on his feet, unharmed. "So," he said, turning to address the other students, "is it good to be bigger and stronger than the other guy when you're doing Jiu-Jitsu? Sure, it's good. But it's not the most important thing. You have to *believe* in the technique for it to work. Believing in the technique is the first step toward mastery. Now, partner up!"

Feeling exhilarated, I started to turn away to find a partner, when Coach Ethan stopped me. "Got it, Nancy?" he said.

"Got it, Coach," I replied, fighting back a smile.

Bess and George came up to me as everyone else broke up to start drilling the move. "Oh my word," Bess said, her eyes alight. "That was so amazing! How did it feel?"

"Pretty awesome," I replied.

"Coach Ethan is *terrifying*," said George.

"Yeah," I agreed. "But in a good way."

"White belts!" Coach Ethan shouted. George nearly jumped out of her skin. "Find a partner before I have everyone in this room doing push-ups! And no white belts with other white belts! You guys can't be trusted with each other. . . ."

George and Bess scrambled to join up with Erica and Jake, both purple belts. I scanned the room. The only student left without a partner was another purple belt named Liam. Liam had copper-colored hair that he'd tied at the back of his head in a small ponytail. He was built like a linebacker and had the rough look of a seasoned fighter, but his cornflower-blue eyes were open and friendly. "Redheads rule," he said, reaching out for a fist bump.

"They certainly do," I said. "Partners?"

"Sure thing, Nancy. Let's do this!"

"Okay, so . . . I throw you, then you throw me?"

He nodded. "First let me show you how to properly

break the fall, and then you can give it a shot. Don't worry, I'm one of the assistant coaches here. I'll let you down gently."

"Sounds good." We started to get into a rhythm, and my throwing—and landings—got a little better with every turn. "So," I said, getting up off the mat for the fifteenth time. "How long have you been doing Jiu-Jitsu?"

Liam put his hands on his hips. "Whew, a long time. Around nine years, I think."

"Wow, that's real dedication. Does it take that long to get a purple belt?"

Liam cleared his throat and looked away. "It's a journey," he said with a pained smile. "Everyone's is different."

"Oh, of course," I said, feeling like I might have put my foot in my mouth. The students here might be pretty competitive about stuff like that. "Do most people come here to learn self-defense?" I asked, trying to change the subject.

"It's a mix," Liam answered, adjusting the knot

on his belt. "Some come for that. Others come to get in shape. And then we have people join who want to become competitors."

"Competitive fighters—that's so cool!" I said. "So, who here competes?"

"A lot of the regulars do," he said. "Carly's been winning a lot of tournaments lately. In fact, she has a big one coming up in a few days, on Saturday. She and some of the others have been training really hard for it."

We spent another fifteen minutes working on the hip toss, and then Coach Ethan gathered everyone to walk us through a few other moves and have us try them out.

"*Time's up!*" Coach Ethan yelled, stopping us in the middle of practicing a defensive technique. "Take a water break, then get your sparring stuff on and partner up! Please find someone of similar size. No bully fights!"

I thanked Liam and gave him another fist bump before jogging to the sidelines and taking a few gulps from my water bottle.

"Wanna roll?"

I turned to see Jamie, a petite girl with a button

nose and dirty-blond hair, looking at me expectantly. "Sure," I said, following her onto the mat. *She's smaller than me, at least,* I thought. *How bad could it be?*

"First time sparring?" she asked. "No worries. Got any brothers?"

"Only child."

"Ever done any high school wrestling?"

"Can't say that I have."

"Ever got in a fight?"

I raised an eyebrow, remembering the untold number of times I'd grappled with thieves, saboteurs, kidnappers, and other criminals, then replied, "More than you'd expect, actually."

"Oh! Well then, sparring should be no problem for you. If you're uncomfortable or anything hurts, just tap out. Easy peasy."

"Easy peasy," I repeated, my heart starting to race as we bumped fists.

"Go!" Coach Ethan shouted, and thus began the most exhausting, confusing, and exhilarating five minutes of my life.

Jamie was a blue belt, so I expected her to be good, but I didn't expect to be so completely and hopelessly outmatched. She moved like a caffeinated puma, while my technique more resembled a hippopotamus encased in Jell-O. Within thirty seconds, I was completely winded, and within a minute, she had my face pressed against the floor. Her legs were twisted around my arm like a pretzel, and with one gentle movement from her, I felt intense pressure in my shoulder. I tapped the mat twice and Jamie released me immediately. By the time I sat up, panting, sweating, and thoroughly impressed, Jamie was already back on her feet.

"What was that?" I asked.

"Omoplata," she replied. "It's a joint lock submission."

"It certainly is," I said, rubbing my shoulder.

"Ready to go again?"

"Again?"

"It's only been two minutes. It's a five-minute match, so we've got three left. You good?"

Was I good? I couldn't really tell. I was tired and sore and maybe a little dizzy, but—

Jamie sensed my indecision. "C'mon, Nancy. You've got a lot of fight in you. I can tell."

I smiled, and suddenly felt a little less tired. "Okay," I said. "Let's go."

Three minutes and two more tap-outs later, I started to understand exactly why people got addicted to this. Being on the other side of that much skill and physical dominance really made you want to know how to do it too.

"Thanks so much," I told Jamie, giving her a fist bump. "That was really fun."

"Anytime!" she said with a smile.

The group took a minute for another water break, and I looked around to see how the girls were doing. George was lying on the floor, hyperventilating. Meanwhile, Erica seemed to be showing Bess how to do some kind of complicated choking technique. "You okay, George?" I called out.

She gave me a thumbs-up, but otherwise didn't move.

"She'll be fine," Jamie assured me. "At least she hasn't thrown up yet!"

"Yet?" I asked nervously.

"Next round, coming up!" Coach Ethan shouted. "Find partners!"

I somehow got through two more sparring rounds—the first with another white belt named Tim, and the last one with Penny. "So, what do you think of Jiu-Jitsu?" Penny asked once our round was over.

"I'll tell you when I catch my breath," I said, struggling to my feet.

Penny laughed.

The class was finished, so we lined up again by belt and bowed out, giving each fellow student a friendly fist bump. As soon as we were done, Bess came running up and grabbed me by the shoulders. "Oh my gosh, Nancy! That was so amazing! I jumped on her, and then she rolled around like *this*, and then I pushed her and she got me in this crazy choke. . . . Erica says I have natural instincts. Can you believe it?"

"Honestly?" I said. "No! You didn't even want to come along tonight!"

"I know, I know. I was just freaked out, but I was *wrong*, Nancy! *So, so wrong!*"

I shook my head in disbelief. Bess Marvin, falling in love with combat sports! Who would have thought? "I'm happy for you. Hey, where's George?"

Bess sucked her teeth. "Well, she left the mat after the second round of sparring and took off for the bathroom. I think she might have been sick."

"Huh," I said, "I guess Jamie was right. . . ."

"Right about what?" Bess asked. "I'd better go check on George—oh! There she is. She looks okay . . . just a little green around the gills."

"Poor George," I said, suppressing a grin. "All her dreams of becoming a ninja dashed by too many cheese fries before training."

As George slowly made her way back to us, Carly jogged over. "So, what did you guys think? Did you have a good time?" she asked.

I opened my mouth to reply, but Bess beat me to

it. "Where do I sign up?" She was practically dancing. "Can I get one of these gi things in pink?"

"Actually," Carly said, "You *can*—"

"*AHH!*"

Everyone in the academy froze as a loud shriek pierced the friendly chatter. It was coming from the lobby. I joined the rest of the group, dashing out of the training area to where Libby was backing away from her desk, her face as pale as a moon.

I followed her eyes to the desk. A large dead rat lay there on its back, its feet stiff and curled, its eyes open and glassy. On the wall behind the desk, someone had spray-painted a single word across the Iron Dragon logo in vivid, dripping red letters:

TRAITOR.

CHAPTER THREE

Martial Law

FOR A MOMENT, THE ROOM WAS QUIET AS we all took in the gruesome tableau. Then everyone started talking at once.

"What the—"

"I think I'm going to be sick. . . ."

"That poor rat!"

"Who did this? Because so help me, I'll—"

Then one voice cut through all the others like a knife. "Let me through."

Everyone fell silent as Coach Ethan made his way to the front of the crowd. He surveyed the damage, his face a mask of barely concealed fury, then turned to Libby. "Explain," he demanded.

"O-okay," Libby stammered. "Well, um—a little while ago, I stepped out to get some cash from the bank, like I usually do on Tuesday and Thursday evenings. I was only gone for five minutes, ten at the most. And when I got back . . ." She gestured toward the dead rat. "It was like this." Her face started to crumple under his harsh stare. "I'm sorry, I never thought—"

Seeing that she was upset, Coach Ethan seemed to soften. "Hey," he said. "It's okay. It's not your fault." His eyes flicked back and forth from the expired rodent to the writing on the wall. "Seems like someone's trying to send us a message. But who? And why?"

I could feel Bess's and George's eyes boring into the back of my head, and when I turned to look, sure enough, my best friends were staring pointedly at me, as if to say, *Well? What are you waiting for?*

All the usual arguments for minding my own business filled my head:

They're better off calling the police.

This isn't your problem.

Don't you have better things to do? Like studying? Or some kind of normal hobby?

I sighed. Who was I kidding? A leopard never changes its spots, and Nancy Drew never turns her back on a mystery.

I cleared my throat. "You don't happen to have any security cameras, do you?" I asked Coach Ethan.

He turned to see who had spoken, and cocked his head in puzzlement when he saw it was me. "Why do you want to know?"

I licked my lips. "Just curious."

"Well, no, I don't," he said, scowling. "Never saw the need for it . . . until now, I guess."

I thought for a moment before saying, "It's likely that this was planned. Clearly, whoever did this knows someone here intimately, especially if they're accusing them of being a traitor. They were probably also famil-iar enough with Libby's routine to know when she'd go out, leaving the lobby empty and unlocked. They knew just how much time they had to get in and out before she got back or class ended—or else risk getting caught."

Coach Ethan crossed his arms, regarding me with interest. "Tell me, Nancy, why do you talk like an undercover cop?"

Chuckling nervously, I shook my head and said, "Not a police officer. Just an amateur detective."

The coach's eyebrows went up. "Are you, now?" he muttered. "So, are you any good?"

"At cracking cases? I have a pretty good track record, yes."

Coach Ethan nodded slowly. Then he turned to the assembled crowd. "All of you, scram! Nancy, come with me."

While the rest of the class went off to the locker rooms to change out of their sweaty gis, I followed Coach Ethan down a hallway and into his office. "Listen," he said once he'd closed the door. "You find the punk who did this, I give you my word: I'll teach you Jiu-Jitsu for free. I'll put a plaque on the door with your name on it. Whatever you want. No one threatens my team and gets away with it."

"You're sure you want to trust me with this responsibility?" I asked. "I mean, you just met me a couple of hours ago."

The head coach chuckled. "I'm a pretty good judge of character. I watched you roll tonight—you're scrappy. Even though you had no idea what you were doing, you worked hard and didn't give up. I like that." He stuck out his hand. "So, do we have a deal?"

I bit my lip. I had a feeling that this mystery wasn't going to be easy to solve. Not only would I have to figure out who the vandal was, I'd need to learn who the message was *for*. Who was the "traitor" in the academy?

I'd already been thrown on the floor more than a dozen times, and that was *before* the case even started. Usually if I got a little banged up, it was as I was closing in on the bad guy. This time, was I biting off more than I could chew?

Nah. Backing down just wasn't part of my DNA. And even though I'd only just met Coach Ethan, I had a pretty good feeling about him, too. I didn't want to let him down.

I took the coach's hand in mine and shook it firmly. "I'll do my best."

Coach Ethan nodded. "That's all I ask," he said.

I followed him out of the office. After a quick change in the locker room, I returned to the lobby, where Carly and Liam were standing by the front desk. He was whispering into her ear, while she stared at the word on the wall, her hands gripped into fists.

Hmm, I wonder what's going on there? I thought.

In the meantime, Libby and some of the other students had been busy gathering supplies to clean the paint off the wall and dispose of the dead rat. I told them to hold off for a second so I could snap a few pictures of it and the graffiti on my phone. "Oh, for evidence?" Tim asked. He was a stocky young guy, with dark copper skin and short black hair.

"Maybe," I replied.

"Cool," he said, rubbing his hands together. "If

they made this into an action movie, they could call it *Danger at the Iron Dragon!*"

Carly and Liam were still standing nearby, whispering. When I was done taking pictures, they walked over to me. "So, Detective Red," Liam said, "are you taking on our case, or what?"

"I am," I said, looking back and forth between them. "Why? Is there something you want to tell me?"

Carly dropped her head. Liam nudged her. "Go on, Carly, she needs to know."

"Yeah, okay, Coach. I'll tell her," she said, all the earlier energy sucked from her voice.

Liam nodded and waved goodbye, following some of the students out. Carly and I walked over to the sitting area and took a seat next to each other on the sofa.

"Nancy!" Bess called to me from the lobby. "You ready to go? George says she needs a smoothie soon or she's going to die." George was slumped in a chair by the door, moaning dramatically.

"I'll be there in a sec!" I replied. "Just keep her alive

for, like, five more minutes!" Bess nodded and gave me a thumbs-up.

I turned back to Carly. "So, what's going on?"

Carly's knee bounced nervously. "It could be nothing, but Liam made me promise to tell you. Whoever wrote that word on the wall did it to scare one of us, right?"

"Right," I said.

"Well," she said, lowering her voice, "I think that person might be me."

I scooched closer and lowered my voice to match hers, so that none of the other students in the lobby nearby could hear us. "What makes you think someone would want to threaten you?"

"So," she began. "Like I told you when we first met, I haven't always trained at Iron Dragon. I started at another academy upstate when I was a kid, but a couple of years ago we moved to River Heights and I needed to find a new team. Back then, I was a blue belt, and another Jiu-Jitsu school a few miles from here courted me: Lockdown MMA. Their academy was really fancy, and their black belt—Brock Vaughn—treated me like royalty when I went to visit. I signed up there, and it was okay for a while. I made some good friends and even started winning local tournaments. But after just a few months, I started noticing things."

I cocked my head. "What kinds of things?"

"Well, first: Brock played favorites, big-time. If you weren't a competitive champion winning medals for the academy, he wouldn't give you the time of day. He rolled out the red carpet for brand-new people, but once they signed a contract, he couldn't care less about them. He just wanted their money. Anyway, I tried to ignore the way he treated the other students and just focus on my own training, but after a while, I couldn't stand it anymore. To me, Jiu-Jitsu is more than just a sport. It teaches you to treat people with respect, no matter who they are. And seeing Brock act that way went against what I believed Jiu-Jitsu is supposed to be about."

"Is that why you left?" I asked.

Her face darkened. "No. I wish I had. But once you're part of an academy, it's not easy to leave your team. No, everything came to a head about six months ago, when I started studying some advanced techniques online and wanted to ask Brock a few questions about them. When I brought the subject up during class, he blew up. Got really angry. Said I was acting like I should run the gym instead of him, and that my tone was disrespectful. It came out of nowhere, but most of the students there are so brainwashed that they didn't think to say anything. After class, I was thinking about how he'd lit into me, and I realized I hadn't really learned anything new since starting at Lockdown. Brock always taught the same fighting system over and over again—the system that he'd made a name for himself with. I was curious, so that night I did some research, and I was shocked at what I found. Not only had he gotten his black belt from a school that no longer existed, but he'd also been written up for suspicious business practices more than once. Some ex-students had even posted online about how he'd forced them to pay hundreds of dollars for their belt promotions. I couldn't believe it. The guy was a total fraud."

Carly sighed heavily, then went on. "The next day when I went to class, I mentioned something about what I'd found out to one of my friends, Lucy Hayes. She was a purple belt, and I trusted her. Well, that was a mistake. Before I knew it, what I'd said had gotten back to Brock. After class, he got me alone in his office and went into full rage mode. He threatened to take my belt and spread rumors about me if I didn't promise to keep quiet. He wanted me to agree to be part of his lies, and said I'd pay if I didn't. But you know—losing a fight is nothing compared to losing your honor. So I left, and I never went back."

I sat back, a little awed. "That was very brave."

Carly snorted and ran her fingers through her tight curls. "I don't know about brave . . . at the time, it felt like the only choice I had. I ended up here at Iron Dragon a few days later. Coach Ethan took me right away. He didn't ask a single question. Not even after some of the students from Lockdown started calling me a *creonte* on social media, just as Brock promised they would. Coach Ethan never blinked an eye. He just told me to ignore them. I was one of the team now, and that's all that mattered."

"A *creonte*?" I asked, rolling the strange word across my tongue. "What's that?"

Carly looked up at me and licked her lips nervously. "It's Jiu-Jitsu slang. For 'traitor.'"

"So, what's our next move?" Bess asked a few minutes later as we were driving home. We'd made a quick stop for smoothies, and I'd just finished filling her and George in on Carly's story.

"I don't know about you," George said from the back seat, "but my next move involves a hot shower and an ice pack."

I chuckled. "Well, at the moment, signs seem to point to Carly as the intended target. She told me she's going to be facing one of her old friends from Lockdown MMA, Lucy Hayes, at the big tournament in a few days, so it's possible that the threat was meant to rattle her before the fight. There are probably students at her old academy who still hold a grudge against her for leaving to train at Iron

Dragon. Knowing how these types of cases usually go, there might be more threats coming, maybe even worse ones, so I told Coach Ethan to have the team keep a close eye on her until the tournament. Meanwhile, we should check out Lockdown for ourselves."

"Ooh, you mean go undercover?" Bess asked.

I nodded. "I thought we could attend a class tomorrow afternoon. Just go in pretending to be new students shopping around for the best Jiu-Jitsu academy in town. We'll be able to talk to Brock Vaughn and hopefully get some information from some of the students who train there."

Bess clapped her hands. "This is so exciting. I've been watching a new show about this supercool secret agent, and she wears the most amazing disguises. This is my chance to channel my inner spy! I'm going to wear my green contacts. Definitely green. Or hazel, do you think? Maybe I can even put in a temporary hair color. How about auburn? Or chestnut?"

"Bess," I said, as I pulled up to her house and put the car in park. "You don't need to wear a disguise. No one at Lockdown has ever seen us before."

But Bess wasn't listening. "My name will be Anastasia Blackstone," she said theatrically, grabbing her bag and opening the door. "Just recently moved here from a little port town in Vermont, daughter of the infamous business tycoon Stanley Blackstone . . ."

"Good night, Bess!" George shouted from the back seat.

Bess huffed and slammed the door, then waved goodbye with a grin.

I glanced at the rearview mirror as I started to back out of the driveway. "You want to come sit up here?"

George propped her feet up on the other back seat, her smoothie cup perched on her lap. "Nope, I'm good. Carry on."

After depositing George, half-asleep, at her house, I finally made my way home. Dad was still awake, gathering up a bunch of files into a box on the kitchen table. A steaming cup of coffee sat beside the box. "Hey, champ!" he said brightly as I walked in. "So? How'd it go tonight?"

"Jiu-Jitsu is really interesting. I like it," I said, setting down my bag. "But I definitely got more than I bargained for. . . ."

Dad picked up his coffee cup and took a sip. "You're kidding. A case? Already?"

I shrugged.

"Well," he said with a sigh. "Guess I'd better put the kettle on again. Go ahead, tell me all about it."

Twenty minutes, two cups of tea, and one sandwich later, Dad was rubbing his chin thoughtfully. "Sounds like an interesting one, Nance. Be careful around these people, though. You don't know who to trust, and most of them are trained fighters. Keep your wits about you."

"Don't worry, I will. What's all this?" I asked, gesturing toward the box of files.

"Just some old court documents from a case I prosecuted a few years back—bank robberies, two in River Heights, and a third in another town nearby."

"Oh yeah?" I said. It was always interesting hearing about my dad's criminal cases. Sometimes it even helped me solve my own. "So, did you win?"

"I did," he said with a nod. "Although the two robbers didn't have much of a chance. Twenty years. Problem is—about a week ago, both of them escaped. They're probably halfway across the country by now, but the police wanted me to pass along any information that might help, so I pulled out my old files. Crazy thing . . ."

"That is crazy. You need any help?"

Dad shook his head. "That's sweet of you, honey, but you should go to bed. You look like you're going to hit the floor any second now."

"Ugh," I moaned, suddenly remembering how many times I *had* hit the floor that night. "You're right. I'm toast. Night, Dad."

I hardly remember the walk upstairs to my room, tossing my bag down on the floor, or the hot shower I took, but at some point, I ended up in bed. I set my alarm to give me an extra hour's sleep, because I was going to need all the rest I could get for the next day.

That was when the real fight would begin—the fight for the truth.

CHAPTER FOUR

~⚬~

Bitter Rivals

You sure you don't want to come? I TEXTED
George the next evening. Last chance.

I'll pass, George replied. Not in the mood to
be thrown on my face 2nite. I'll do some digging online on BJJ stuff and report back. k?

OK, I texted back, with a winky emoji. I looked up
from where I was sitting in my car and saw that Bess
had just parked. Gotta go. Looks like Anastasia
Blackstone has arrived.

George sent back an eye-rolling emoji. I laughed,
then tossed my phone into my bag as Bess walked

toward my car. I got out and met her on the side-walk.

"Why, hello, Katarina," she said, giving me a little wave.

I raised an eyebrow. "Excuse me?"

"Katarina White. That's your undercover name," she said.

"What are we supposed to be? Russian princesses?"

Bess clucked her tongue. "We can't give them our *real* names, obviously. The secret agent on that show has a different name in every episode. According to her, 'A good code name is the first rule of spying.'"

I studied her overlarge sunglasses and the brightly colored silk scarf wrapped around her head. "Actually, the first rule of spying is: don't look like a spy."

"Oh, fine," Bess said, pulling off the scarf and glasses. "Sometimes you really are a party pooper, Nancy. You should be happy I didn't have enough time to dye my hair. But honestly, we should really use the names! The River Heights Jiu-Jitsu community is probably pretty small—word could get around that

Nancy Drew is on the case. I thought you wanted to go incognito."

I considered this for a moment and relented. "Okay, you've got a point. We're Ana and Kat, two newbies just looking to learn some Jiu-Jitsu. Got it?"

"Got it."

I narrowed my eyes at her. "You're not going to act weird, right?"

"*Moi?*" Bess asked, looking offended. "*Mais non!*"

Oh man, I thought, shaking my head. *She's totally going to act weird.*

Lockdown MMA was in an upscale section of River Heights, and the facility was large and sleek, with expensive-looking furniture in the lobby and high-energy rock music filtering in through hidden speakers. A poster on one wall showed a large, imposing man with a shaved head dressed in a black gi. Beside him, in bold white letters, read: LEARN PURE JIU-JITSU FROM THE UNDEFEATED MASTER: BROCK VAUGHN. LOCKDOWN MMA IS THE ONLY PLACE YOU CAN BECOME A CHAMPION!

"This is . . . different," Bess murmured.

I nodded. The place was really nice, but at the same time, it seemed like it was trying too hard. Compared to this academy, Iron Dragon felt much more modest, despite the dozens of trophies and medals that were displayed in their lobby next to Libby's desk.

A moment later Brock Vaughn himself emerged from a hallway, looking like he had stepped right out of the poster on the wall. His black gi had a Lockdown patch on the sleeve: a keyhole forming the letter *O* with the silhouette of a gorilla in the background. "Ladies!" he announced. "What brings you in today?"

"Um, hello!" I said, craning my neck to look up at him. He must have been at least six foot five. "We're interested in doing a trial class."

He smiled, showing all his teeth. "Well, you've just made the best decision of your lives." He reached out to shake both our hands vigorously. "I'm Master Brock Vaughn, third-degree black belt and world champion fighter. I'll be guiding you on your Jiu-Jitsu journey. Now, come with me." He ushered us farther

into the reception area, where a few other employees popped up from desks like prairie dogs to help
us. "First we'll have you sign a couple of waivers, and
then we'll get you both some official Lockdown uni-
forms to try on!"

The next half hour was very similar to our experience at Iron Dragon. We got dressed and joined the
dozen students already waiting for the class to start in
an airy training room, then went through a similarly
challenging warm-up that left me breathless.

"This case is exhausting," I muttered to Bess when
we were done.

"I know!" she squealed. "Isn't it awesome?"

"All right, everyone, circle up!" Master Brock commanded, and the students quickly gathered in the center of the mats. "We're going over armbars today. Lucy,
come out."

A purple-belt girl with blue eyes and light brown
hair tied in a messy ponytail jumped to her feet to help
Master Brock demonstrate the technique. "That must
be Lucy Hayes," I whispered in Bess's ear. "The girl

Carly told me about—the friend who ratted her out to Master Brock."

"She looks like she means business," Bess replied.

I had to agree. Lucy wasn't particularly big or tall, but her intense expression throughout the demonstration made it clear she wasn't someone to mess with.

Master Brock began by showing us the various details of the move, which was a joint lock meant to put intense pressure on the elbow. "The secret to armbars is speed and accuracy!" he said. "You're applying the strength of your entire body against your opponent's one arm. Do it correctly, and they have no chance against you! Now, partner up for drilling."

I scanned the room. Bess ended up with Lucy, which was good, but all the other students were big, intimidating young men who didn't look even slightly interested in drilling with me. Finally my gaze landed on a skinny guy about my age, with light brown skin, black hair, and a goatee. Unlike the rest of the students, his face radiated friendliness. I walked over to him, and as soon as he saw me, his eyes lit up.

"Hi, I'm Na—um, I mean, Kat," I said, holding out my hand.

"Hey, I'm Zhuang," he replied, giving me a firm handshake. He seemed surprised for some reason—maybe they didn't usually have a lot of girls at this academy? "Zhuang Ha, but my friends call me Z. You ready to do some armbars, dude?"

"Ready when you are," I said, smiling.

Turns out, armbars are a lot more difficult than they look. During my go, I swiveled around awkwardly, trying to get the right angle, but nothing I did seemed to work. Strangely, when Master Brock walked by and saw what a mess I was making of the technique, all he said was, "Looking good, Kat! You're a natural!"

Hmm, I thought, *maybe this is what Carly was talking about when she said all Brock is interested in is people's money. Even though I'm doing the technique wrong, he probably wants to make me feel good so I'll sign a contract.*

After a few more minutes of practice, it seemed safe to start asking a few probing questions. "So," I said, grimacing as Z pulled my wrist back until I had to tap. "How long have you been training here?"

"About a year or so," he answered.

I clambered into position to try out another arm-bar. "Wow!" I said, panting. "So you like this academy? How does it compare to the other ones in River Heights?"

Z tapped on my shoulder as I managed to finish the submission. "Why do you want to know?"

"Well, my friend and I want to learn Jiu-Jitsu, but we haven't decided where we want to train yet. We've also been looking at Iron Dragon."

Z sat up and glanced side to side to see if any of the other pairs were close enough to hear us. "I wouldn't say that name too loud around here, if I were you."

I wiped a bead of sweat from my eye and tried not to look overly interested. "Oh? Why not?"

"Let's just say the vibe between Lockdown and Iron Dragon isn't super chill."

"Did something happen to make the vibe . . . not . . . chill?" I asked, wincing at my own lack of coolness.

Z looked at me curiously. "You sure do ask a lot of questions . . . *Kat*."

"Just nosy, I guess," I said, shrugging. The last thing I needed was to have my cover blown before I got any information!

A moment later my head began to swim. The combination of fatigue, nervousness, and the craziness of the past two days was making me light-headed. I needed a minute to put myself together—passing out on the floor in the middle of class was definitely *not* incognito. "Hey, I have to use the restroom. Do you mind?"

"No problem," Z said.

"Thanks. I'll be right back!" I jogged off the mat, heading toward the women's locker room at the back of the building.

There, I splashed some cold water on my face and gave myself a few minutes to get my bearings. Z had seemed a little suspicious when I'd mentioned Iron Dragon—could it be that he knew something? I'd have to be careful not to let on that I was connected with Carly Griffith, or else everyone in this place could clam up pretty quickly. *You can do this,* I told myself. *Just be cool. Subtle. Not "Anastasia Blackstone" subtle. Actually subtle.*

I took a couple of deep breaths and opened the door, ready to get back into drilling. But when I walked out into the hallway, someone was there waiting for me.

"Z!" I said, surprised. "Is everything okay? I was just—"

He regarded me with narrowed eyes. "You're not who you say you are," he said in a low voice. "Are you . . . Nancy Drew?"

CHAPTER FIVE

~

The Heat Is On

HOW DID HE KNOW MY NAME?

"Nancy who?" I said, feigning confusion. I had to try to keep up my cover story, or else my newest case would be dead in the water. "I'm just here to try a class. I don't know who you think I am, but—"

But Z wasn't buying it. He took a step closer to me, his dark eyes piercing. "Nancy Drew, only daughter of local prosecutor Carson Drew," Z rattled off. "Amateur detective. Has solved countless cases in the River Heights area and beyond. Partners include cousins Bess Marvin and George Fayne—I'm guessing that's

Bess who tagged along with you tonight?"

I felt my jaw drop. "Uh," I managed.

The mission has been compromised, I thought. *Abort! Abort!*

I was about to push past Z and make a run for it when he reached out and grabbed my hand, pumping it up and down. "It's an honor to meet you, Ms. Drew. I'm such a big fan!"

I blinked in surprise. "Wait . . . what? A fan? Of me?"

"Totally!" Z replied, his entire face transformed by a huge smile. "I knew it was you the moment you walked in! I was confused at first because of the whole 'Kat' thing, but then I realized you must be *undercover*." He said the last word in a whisper.

"Wow," I said, heaving a sigh of relief. "You scared the heck out of me, Z. I thought you were going to try to beat me up or something."

Z's eyes widened. "Me? Beat up Nancy Drew?" He laughed. "Dude, I'd never. I was just so jazzed to meet you, and I wanted a chance to talk to you alone without giving away the game."

"But how do you know about me? All those details?" I asked.

Z reached up to fix his hair, which was sticking straight up like a coxcomb after all the armbars. "Oh, I'm a junior reporter for the *River Heights Bugle*. I've seen your photograph in some back issues and read all the articles about you. It's great stuff! Much more exciting than the high school sports scores and reports from city council meetings I usually have to cover. Anyway . . ." He glanced over his shoulder to make sure we were still alone. "What's the scoop, Nancy? Stolen trophy? Black-belt blackmail? Some other kind of Jiu-Jitsu crime?"

I bit my lip. I wanted to keep the details of this case under wraps, but on the other hand, having a local reporter on my side—with access to all kinds of information—might come in handy. Maybe I could use this new development to my advantage. . . . "If I tell you about the case," I said carefully, "you have to *promise* to keep it to yourself. It's really important."

Z nodded and threw his shoulders back like a

trained soldier. "Totally understand. Lives are at stake. The fate of the world. You can count on me."

"I mean, the 'fate of the world' might be overstating it a bit—"

"You never know . . ." Z's eyes were sparkling.

He was really enjoying this. *And who am I to argue with him?* I thought. *I'm a girl who solves mysteries for fun.*

I smiled. "You're right—lives *are* at stake. Welcome to the team, Z." I pulled out my phone and brought up the photos I'd taken of the dead rat and the graffiti. "Take a look," I said, turning the screen toward him. "Someone snuck into Iron Dragon MMA last night and did this. I'm following up on a lead that one of the people here at Lockdown might be trying to intimidate Carly Griffith. She's got a big competition coming up, and she's going to be fighting some of her old teammates. You're a student here. Do you think anyone on Team Lockdown would ever do something like this?"

Z rubbed his chin. "Hmm. It *was* a big deal when Carly left. I heard that she made a bunch of accusations against Master Brock—I never heard any of them myself—and he was *not happy* about it. Said it was all made up, and that a liar like her didn't belong in his academy. Master Brock led us to believe that he kicked her out after that. Are you saying that she split on her own?"

"That's what Carly told me," I replied. "She said that she'd found some pretty convincing evidence that Brock was a fraud and told Lucy Hayes about it. But instead of keeping the secret, Lucy went and told Brock—which must have led to the confrontation you heard about. Carly said that he told her to take back what she said or pay the price. So she decided to leave." I shook my head. "Seems to me that Master Brock might be the liar."

Z looked surprised. "Dang. That's a real different story from the one I'd heard. I really believed in Master Brock. . . . If what you're saying is true, he really isn't the guy I thought he was."

I looked at the floor. "I'm really sorry to be the bearer of bad news, Z."

"Hey, no—it's okay. Better to know the truth, right?"

I nodded. "So, with that in mind: Do you think Lucy or Brock could have done this?"

"People are crazy, man," said Z with a shrug. "If I learned anything from reading those articles about you, it's that even if you *think* you know someone, you probably don't. Not really. I mean, Lucy was always a little jealous of Carly's success, and if Brock threatened Carly like you said he did, both of them have a pretty good reason to try to scare her off."

So they've both got means and motive, I thought. *But what about opportunity?*

"Can you tell me when the last class here at Lockdown ended last night?" I asked.

"Ten o'clock. Brock and Lucy were both here. We all left at the same time."

That's half an hour before we were done with class at Iron Dragon. And Lockdown's only a ten-minute drive away. It's possible that either Lucy or Brock could have been there in time to leave the rat and the tag.

I smiled. Things were starting to get interesting. "Good to know. Thanks, Z," I said. I glanced back toward the main room, where Master Brock was announcing that it was time to spar. "We'd better get back before we're missed. Hey, would it be okay if I kept in touch with you? If you're here every night, you might see something that could be helpful. Plus, it's always good for a detective to have a friend in the press. . . ."

Z positively glowed. "Dude, you don't even have to ask. Anything you need, anytime! Just keep me in mind when this thing starts to heat up. Nothing like a front-page story to make a junior reporter get noticed in the newsroom."

"You got it."

He raised his fist, and I gave it a bump.

After three rounds of sparring, Bess and I dragged ourselves outside, sore and exhausted.

"This is starting to feel like a habit," I groaned. I'd thrown back on my black tights and gray River Heights High sweatshirt, and I desperately needed a shower. After making sure that none of the other students were nearby, I quickly filled Bess in on my conversation with Z.

"Oh! A reporter. That's good," she said. "Meanwhile, Anastasia Blackstone risked her life to retrieve vital information. I rolled with *Lucy Hayes*." She tossed her head, which usually looks good, given Bess's flowing blond locks, but she was so soaked in sweat that she looked more like a drowned cat than a diva.

"Oh my," I said, trying to keep a straight face. "And pray tell, what did Anastasia Blackstone find out?"

"Well, when she shared that she was a competitive fighter, I asked her all sorts of questions about it, and she told me about that upcoming tournament and who she's fighting. Carly is one of her opponents—they're the same belt, same weight class and division. When she mentioned Carly's name, she looked nervous—like maybe she was hiding something. I probed a little bit, and she told me that they'd been really good friends once. I actually felt kind of sad for her. But at the same time, isn't it the people closest to us who can hurt us the most?"

I sighed. "Unfortunately, yes. The closer the two girls were before they fell out, the more likely it is that Lucy might want revenge on Carly for abandoning her team. Even if Carly had a good reason to leave."

Bess grabbed my arm. "Oh, and get this! I noticed while we were rolling that Lucy had red paint on some of her fingernails."

"It could just be some leftover nail polish," I reasoned.

"Maybe," Bess said, raising an eyebrow. "*Or it could be spray paint from when she vandalized Iron Dragon!*"

"You're right, it could," I said with a nod. "Nice work, Anastasia. Things at Lockdown are definitely looking suspicious." I yawned. "But right now, I'm ready for bed. Call you tomorrow?"

"*Parfait!*" Bess replied, tossing her gym bag into her car. "*Bonne nuit, ma chère!*"

"I'm confused," I said. "I thought we were from Vermont. Or Russian princesses?"

Bess shrugged. "I don't know any Russian."

"Then why— Oh, never mind." I shook my head and waved before getting into my own car and taking off toward home.

A few minutes later I was stopped at a red light less than a block from Iron Dragon, listening to the radio and thinking about everything I'd learned so far. At first I'd thought that this case was going to be tough to crack—there were so many unanswered questions at the start—but I seemed to be getting the answers I needed pretty easily.

Maybe this won't be as hard as I thought. Wouldn't that be a first!

As I drove past Iron Dragon MMA, I happened to glance through the window and saw something strange: a light inside the darkened building, moving around erratically. The beam against the walls was round, like from a flashlight. I checked the dashboard clock. Ten thirty p.m. Libby had said that the academy was closed on Wednesdays except for private lessons, and it was hard to believe someone would be still be hanging around at this time of night. And in the dark? What was going on in there?

Then I remembered something I'd said that first night: *There might be more threats coming, maybe even worse ones.* I gripped the steering wheel. Was it dangerous and possibly a little stupid to go check things out? Yup. Would Dad kill me if he found out? Definitely. Despite all the alarm bells signaling that I should just continue on home, was I going to pull over and go investigate? Absolutely.

Sixty seconds later, after parking the car, I was sneaking up the sidewalk toward Iron Dragon, armed with nothing but curiosity and a big, heavy wrench I'd found in the trunk. Pressing myself up against the wall of the building, I peeked into the window. At first I didn't see anything. Had my eyes been playing tricks on me? Maybe it was nothing. . . .

But then I spied a light growing inside—though it looked different from what I'd seen before. Instead of the bright beam of a flashlight, this was a yellow flicker coming from the hallway that led to Coach

Ethan's office. I was trying to figure out what it could be, when an unmistakable smell struck my nose.

Smoke.

Oh my word, I thought. *Iron Dragon is on fire!*

For the second time that week, I fumbled with my phone to call 911.

"What's your emergency?" the dispatcher answered.

"There's a fire inside the Iron Dragon MMA building downtown," I said. "At the intersection of Allen Street and Mueller Avenue. Please come quickly!"

"We'll be there right away, miss! Do you know if there's anyone inside?"

I thought about the flashlight, then said, "I don't know. There might be."

"Okay. Fire and ambulance services will be there soon. Whatever you do, don't go inside!"

I hung up the phone and peered through the window again. The fire was spreading. I could see it climbing up the walls and across the carpet like a hungry animal, feeding and growing stronger as it burned.

Suddenly a figure stumbled out of the hallway

and into the dark lobby. The person leaned against the doorframe for a moment before collapsing to the floor.

I felt all the blood drain from my face. Whoever that was, they were in terrible danger!

Whatever you do, don't go inside, the dispatcher had said. I searched the street both ways, but there was no sign of the fire trucks or ambulances yet. I turned back to the window, and my heart raced as I saw the fire licking closer and closer to the body.

There was no time to wait. If I didn't get in there right away, they'd never make it out!

I tried the door, but it was locked. I was about to try kicking it in, when I remembered the heavy wrench in my hand. Taking a step back, I brought it down as hard as I could against the tempered glass door, instantly shattering it into a million pieces. I carefully slipped my hand through to unlock the door, then pushed it open, my shoes crunching on the shards as I rushed into the building.

I coughed violently as I took in a lungful of the

billowing black smoke rolling through the lobby. Dropping to the floor, I pulled my T-shirt up over my mouth and army-crawled as quickly as I could over to the body. Even with the person facing away from me, I knew from the red hair exactly who it was.

Liam!

The assistant coach was dressed in jeans and a T-shirt, and his hair was sticky with blood. I pressed my fingers to the side of his neck and was relieved to feel a strong pulse there. "Liam!" I shouted, shaking him. "Wake up! We've got to get out of here!"

He didn't stir.

Meanwhile, the fire was moving closer to us every second. Burning overhead, the inferno had created a rippling blanket of heat; I could feel the top of my hair singeing. I'd have to drag Liam out of the building—and fast—or we were both toast.

Staggering to my feet, I grabbed Liam's limp body by the armpits and started inching him across the floor toward the exit. He probably weighed close to two hundred pounds, but he might as well have weighed a ton. I started panting from the effort, but every breath meant choking on the thick smoke.

Slow, shallow breaths, I told myself. *You're almost there.*

The door seemed miles away. My eyes stung, watering from the soot; I squeezed them shut and kept moving one painful inch at a time.

When I opened them again, the door was only a few feet away.

Just a little farther . . .

With one last herculean heave, I dragged Liam's deadweight through the shattered front door to the sidewalk outside, not stopping until we were a safe distance from the building. Then I fell gasping to the pavement next to him, the cool night air like a balm to my burning skin.

We made it, I thought. *We're alive.* A few seconds later I heard the distant blare of sirens and breathed a sigh of relief. Hopefully, they'd get here in time to save Iron Dragon, too.

Sitting up, I tried to rub my stinging eyes but

quickly realized that my hands were coated in a thin film of ash, as was everything else. Instead I pulled a tissue from my pocket and used that to wipe my face, so at least I'd be able to see properly. As I blinked rapidly, my eyes focused on the now-visible flames lighting up the inside of the academy.

But then something else caught my attention. Movement in the alleyway between two buildings. Craning my neck, I saw a figure sneaking out the back door of Iron Dragon before taking off down the dark alley.

That head wound looks nasty. Someone must have knocked Liam out, I thought. *And fires don't usually start themselves. . . .*

I struggled to my feet, every muscle crying out for relief.

No rest for the weary, I thought, and took off after the mysterious shadow.

CHAPTER SIX

~

Grappling with the Truth

I RACED INTO THE DARKNESS. MY LUNGS burned as I ran, but I tried to ignore the pain and concentrate on not tripping over the garbage cans that jammed the narrow alleyway. As my pounding footsteps got closer, the figure must have heard me on their heels, because they glanced over their shoulder. I studied the face, but it was much too dark to make out any identifying features. All I could tell was that the person had an average build and was wearing jeans and some kind of hooded jacket.

As soon as the person caught sight of me, they

grabbed the nearest garbage can and upended it, sending the foul-smelling contents spilling everywhere. I lost a few seconds as I struggled to push the metal can out of the way. When I looked up again, the alley was empty.

Where did they go?

After ten more yards the alley split three ways, following the lines of the neighboring buildings. I scanned each route, looking for any sign of the figure, but they were gone.

Then, in the left-hand branch, I saw it: a puddle from a rainstorm earlier in the day. The water rippled as if someone had splashed through it just seconds before. *Gotta be this way,* I thought, before taking off down that route.

Moments later I knew my hunch had been right. I turned a corner and caught sight of the hooded figure up ahead, scaling a chain-link fence. "Hey!" I shouted. "Stop!" Instead, the person climbed faster, straddling the top of the fence and snagging their jacket on it in the process. I heard the sound of fabric ripping and thought I saw something small and square drop out of a pocket as they struggled to get untangled. By the time I hit the fence, they'd already jumped down on the other side and bolted.

Taking a deep breath, I grabbed onto the chain-link and hoisted myself up. I might not be the most graceful climber in the world, but I made it to the top in record time—especially considering how tired I was. It's amazing what a little adrenaline can do! Gingerly avoiding the poky parts at the top, I leaped down and landed in a squat among a scattering of windblown trash, then tore out of the alley, which opened out onto another darkened street lined with shuttered shops and parked cars. Squinting into the gloom, I searched for any movement, but once again, the figure was nowhere to be seen.

I'd lost the suspect.

"Darn!" I muttered, kicking an empty bottle down the sidewalk. I'd been so close!

I started to double back to Iron Dragon, but then I turned around, picked up the bottle, and tossed it into a nearby garbage can. What can I say? Nancy Drew may be a little slow on her feet, but she's no litterbug!

As I brushed the dirt off my hands, I remembered the object that had fallen out of the person's pocket as they were scaling the fence. I had to try to find it. Maybe it would help me work out their identity or what they'd been up to.

I returned to the fence and climbed back over, more carefully this time. Once I was safely on the other side again, I yanked out my phone and pulled up the flashlight app, casting the glow across the ground. There wasn't much there: a few candy bar wrappers, some empty soda cans—and a green matchbox.

"Well, hello," I said, bending to pick up the matchbox. I held it close to the light to get a better look. Below an illustration of a hand of playing cards were the words CRAZY EIGHTS. I shook the box. It sounded about half full. Probably enough matches missing to start a pretty good fire. Pushing the matchbox into my pocket, I made my way back to Iron Dragon as quickly as I could.

By the time I'd navigated the maze of alleys back to

the academy, most of the excitement seemed to be over. It looked like the fire was out. I could see half a dozen firefighters inside the lobby, moving damaged furniture and searching for anything still burning. Liam was sitting on the curb next to an ambulance, wrapped in a silver blanket and breathing through an oxygen mask. A gauze bandage was secured around his head with medical tape, but apart from some soot smeared across his face, he looked okay.

A young, uniformed police officer with bronze-colored skin a short beard was talking to him. The officer looked up as I approached.

"Are you the young lady who called 911?" he asked. The name tag above his badge read NADEEM.

I nodded. "Is the academy going to be all right?" I asked.

"It is, thanks to you," he replied. "Fire services got here just in time to contain the blaze before it really got going. Another ten minutes, and it might have taken the whole building down. And I'm sure this fellow with it."

Liam looked up at me and blinked. "N-Nancy?" he stammered. "*You* pulled me out of the building? But how? What are you doing here?"

"It was luck, really," I said. "I just happened to be driving by on my way home and I saw some strange lights inside the academy. When I got closer to make sure everything was okay, I saw the fire—and you."

Liam's eyes went wide. As he stood up shakily, the silver blanket slipped from his shoulders. "Oh my word. You saved my life," he said, grasping my shoulder. "I don't know what to say."

Officer Nadeem leaned over. "'Thank you' might be a good start, my friend."

"Oh, uh, of course," Liam said, his cheeks going pink. "Thank you, Nancy. Thank you so much!"

I shrugged. "It's what any good person would have done." I turned to the police officer. "By the way, after I got us out, I saw someone leaving through the back door. I chased them down the alleys, but I couldn't get a good look at their face before they got away. I did find this, though." I pulled the matchbox out of my pocket and handed it to the officer. "It makes me think this was arson."

Officer Nadeem studied the matchbox, and then me. "First you run into a burning building, and then you chase a suspect through this part of the city in the pitch dark?" He cocked his head, his face curious. "Who are you, young lady?"

I stood a little taller, a grin pulling at the corner of my lips. "I'm Nancy Drew."

The officer smiled. "I see. A bit of a detective yourself, are you?"

"You could say that."

"Well, Nancy Drew," he said, peering at the matchbox, "if you don't mind sticking around for a few minutes, I'd like to take a statement from you."

"Of course," I said, and told him everything that had happened, including all about the rat incident the night before.

Officer Nadeem scribbled everything down in his notebook before flipping it closed. "Well, that helps a lot, Miss Drew. Thank you. I'll take this evidence to my superiors and include the information you provided in my report."

"Oh, can I take a photo of it first?" I asked, pointing at the matchbox.

"I guess so . . . ," Officer Nadeem said, handing it to me. "But don't even think about getting involved in this, young lady. Leave the crime solving to the professionals, please."

"Yes, sir," I said, not meeting his eyes.

I snapped a couple of pictures of the matchbox with my phone before handing it back to the officer.

As Officer Nadeem went over to consult with the other police officers on the scene, I turned back to Liam. "I'm glad you're okay. I was so worried. But what were you doing at the academy so late?"

Unsteady on his feet, Liam sank back down on the curb, wincing. "I'd had a couple of private lessons earlier in the evening, and I stayed to finish entering some membership data into the computer in the office. I was at it for about half an hour when I heard a noise and got up to check it out. The second I walked out of the office door, someone hit me. I didn't go down right away, though—I stumbled through the hall to try to get help, but I didn't make it far before I collapsed. That must have been when you saw me."

I nodded. "Try to remember, Liam—did you see or hear *anything* that might help us figure out who did this to you? I have a feeling that whoever hit you and started the fire is the same person who left that dead rat in the academy last night."

Deep concern crossed Liam's face. "Really? Are you sure?"

"I can't be absolutely certain," I said. "But it makes sense. Someone is threatening Iron Dragon and one of its members. I have some ideas on who and why . . . but I'm still exploring different possibilities. That's why I really need to know if you saw anything."

Liam pressed his lips together and sighed. "I don't know," he said after a moment, running his fingers through his messy hair. "Everything happened so fast, and I was barely conscious. But I think I might have seen something on the back of the person's jacket. Some kind of logo."

"Go on," I urged. "Think back. . . ."

He closed his eyes, concentrating. "An animal, maybe? Yeah, it had a dark, thick body and arms and a big head. A bear, maybe? Or an ape?" He shook his head. "That's all I've got. I don't know if that helps at all. I'm sorry."

"No, that's good," I reassured him. "Anything helps. Have you been cleared by the paramedics to drive home?"

Liam nodded.

"Then you should go get some rest," I said, helping him back to his feet. "You've had a long night."

"It sounds like you have too. Thanks again for what you did."

Once I got Liam safely into his car, I walked back to the academy, where Officer Nadeem was standing guard at the door while the firefighters finished up their work. The dark clouds of smoke that had been billowing out the door had cleared, and surprisingly, the academy didn't look too bad. One of the walls and a big section of the ceiling and carpet were blackened and melted, but that was pretty much it. What a relief!

My body was yelling at me to go lie down, some-where—anywhere—but I wasn't done for the night. Not quite yet.

"Excuse me, officer," I said.

Officer Nadeem looked up at me, puzzled. "Hello again! You're still here. . . . Can I help you?"

"Yes, I think I left something of mine inside," I lied. "Would you mind if I went in to get it?"

Officer Nadeem crossed his arms over his chest and gave me a stern look. "You wouldn't be trying to snoop around, would you?"

"Me?" I said, feigning shock. "Of course not. I just wanted to grab my things and—"

"I'm afraid it isn't safe to come in at the moment," he said, cutting me off. "Not until the firefighters clear the area. You'll have to get your things tomorrow. Good night, Miss Drew." His last words had an edge of finality.

I nodded, giving the officer a smile and a wave. My smile turned into a grimace as soon as I had my back to him. *I have to check the place for evidence. If I don't find a way inside tonight, someone might move something important before I can come back.* With Officer Nadeem standing guard at the door, and three firefighters still working inside, that wasn't going to be easy.

Unless . . .

Why not get in the same way the dark figure had gotten out?

I made my way through the alley and found the back door to the academy slightly ajar. It had a sticky latch, and the suspect must not have closed it all the way earlier when they fled. *All the better for me,* I thought with satisfaction, and slipped quietly inside.

The smell of smoke in the dark training room almost made me cough, but I managed to stifle the sound in my sleeve. I stuck to the shadows, unmoving, and took in the scene. The three firefighters were up in the lobby where the fire had started, and luckily had their backs to me. Unfortunately, that meant that

I wouldn't be able to check the lobby or the office, but hey, it was better than nothing.

Careful not to make a sound, I switched on the flashlight on my phone and searched the training room, looking for anything out of place. Nothing. Next I snuck into the men's locker room, but I didn't find anything there, either. Finally I slipped into the women's locker room.

Again, everything looked normal. I was about to give up and head home when my foot landed on something hard and sharp lying on the floor. "Ouch!" I muttered, and cast my light down to see what it was.

A broken padlock.

I picked it up, walked over to the wall of lockers, and began inspecting each one. They were all labeled with names, written in black marker. Out of the fifteen doors, only one was missing a lock—Penny's. Inside, her locker was a mess. It looked like someone had rummaged through it. I wondered what they'd been looking for, and if they'd found it.

I rubbed my chin, suddenly very confused. Why

would anyone break into *Penny's* locker? I remembered sparring with her the night before. She was a white belt and fairly new to the sport, so I couldn't imagine someone going to all this trouble to threaten her. Was she even fighting in the upcoming tournament? No, it didn't make any sense.

I studied the lockers again and noticed that Carly's was right next to Penny's. Was it possible that the intruder had mistakenly robbed the wrong locker? The room was dark, and they were probably in a hurry, so . . . maybe? But why break into her locker at all? Was there something important in there, or even something they could use to blackmail Carly? I made a mental note to ask her about it the next day.

Voices outside the locker room brought me out of my speculation, and I quickly shut off my light and snuck back out into the training room. The firefighters were still chatting in the lobby.

But as the locker room door closed, it let out a loud creak. The voices cut off abruptly.

"Did you hear something?"

I froze, not daring even to breathe.

"Nah, probably just stuff shifting around," a different firefighter replied. "Always happens after a fire."

I exhaled, then hurried out the back door, avoiding the glances of the police officers as I made my way to my car.

I should have felt victorious—after all, I'd saved someone's life, stopped the academy from burning down, and found two new pieces of evidence in the case. So . . . why did I feel so troubled?

You're just tired, I told myself. *Everything will make more sense in the morning.* I shook my head, trying to clear it. Somehow, even though I'd left the fire far behind, I still felt like I was walking through a house full of smoke.

CHAPTER SEVEN

Going to the Mat

"NANCY."

The voice sounded so far away. I was in a dark, quiet place. It was so nice there.

"Nancy!"

Why won't they leave me alone? I nuzzled deeper into the warm softness all around me.

"Nancy, wake up!"

I heard curtain rings sliding across a rod, and the comfortable darkness was shattered by a blast of light that burned through my eyelids. Groaning, I opened my eyes and saw Bess's grinning face only inches from my own.

"Time to get up, sleepyhead!" she sang. "I can hardly believe you're still in bed! It's past nine!" Her loose hair glowed golden in the sunlight. She looked annoyingly awake and fresh in her pale blue cotton dress.

"I can hardly believe you're getting both of us up this early," George grumbled from across the room. She was dressed in jeans, an army-green T-shirt, and high-tops, and was splayed out in the armchair I keep by the window, a steaming mug in her hand.

"I can't help it!" Bess said. "This case has got me all excited. I thought we should get together and share notes before we start on the day."

"Is that coffee?" I asked, sitting up in bed. Apparently, it was the wrong move, because the minute I tried to stand up, every single part of my body screamed out in pain. "Auggghhhh," I moaned, slumping back into bed.

"Here," Bess said, handing over a mug for me. "This will make you feel better." She wrinkled her nose as she passed by the heap of clothes I'd tossed on the floor in the early hours before crawling under the covers. "Nancy, why does everything smell like smoke?"

I took a sip of coffee and sighed. "Oh, probably because I had to pull a guy out of a burning building last night."

George almost choked on her coffee. Bess's eyes went wide. "A burning building?" she said. "But everything was fine when I left you last night! What happened?"

I spent the next ten minutes filling them in about the fire at Iron Dragon, the chase through the alleys, and what Liam had said about his attacker. They were riveted through it all, their coffees growing cold in their hands.

"What a story!" George said when I was finished.

Bess looked thoughtful. "Did you say Liam saw a logo of an ape on the attacker's jacket?" she asked.

I nodded. "An ape or a bear. He wasn't sure. It was a large animal with dark fur. That's all he could really remember."

Bess set down her cup and pulled her phone from her pocket. She tapped at the screen for a moment before turning it to face me. "You mean something like this?"

I looked at the image and gasped. Displayed on the screen was a black silhouette of a hulking gorilla—the

Lockdown logo. "How could I have forgotten?" I exclaimed, covering my face with my hands.

"Maybe because you were too busy chasing criminals through the streets and suffering from smoke inhalation." George slapped me on the back. "Cut yourself some slack, Nance. You can't think of everything. That's why you have us."

I smiled. "You're right. Thanks, team."

"Three brains are better than one! Even if that one belongs to Nancy Drew," Bess said with a wink. I blushed.

"So, what's our next move?" George asked.

I set my coffee cup on the nightstand and grabbed my phone. "I think I'll get in touch with my contact over at Lockdown and see who doesn't have an alibi."

I quickly tapped out a text to Z, asking him where everyone on the team had been at about half past ten last night. It took only about ten minutes to get from Lockdown to Iron Dragon—but whoever was responsible was already in the building by the time I passed there at ten thirty.

After a minute or so, Z replied.

After you left, everyone went down the street for pizza. We were all there until about 11.

Everyone? I wrote back. Including Lucy and Master Brock?

Yeah, dude, he wrote. Master Brock destroyed a large pepperoni pie. I saw it with my own eyes. I think someone posted pics on social media if you want to check. Z had included a pizza-slice emoji and the shifty eyes emoji along with his message.

I thanked him and dropped the phone on the bed. "Well," I said, resting my chin in my hand. "So much for that theory. . . ."

"What happened?" Bess asked.

"It's no good. All my suspects at Lockdown were at a pizza joint during the fire. None of them could be our arsonist."

"They could have hired someone else to do their dirty work," George suggested.

I collapsed back onto my pillow and stared at the

ceiling. "Yeah, it's possible. But it's also frustrating and messy. If Brock or Lucy hired some thug to set the academy on fire, it's not going to be easy for us to find proof. We'd basically have to be there to catch them in the act. And I can't be at Lockdown watching their every move. . . ."

"I have an idea," Bess said. "One that involves a girl named Anastasia Blackstone." She waggled her eyebrows.

George rolled her eyes. "Not this again."

"Actually," I said, "that's perfect!" I eased my sore body out of bed and started to pace the room. "You'll be my mole, Bess. You can go to Lockdown, tell Brock you're considering signing up but want to try it a few more times, take a bunch of classes, and sniff around for more information. I trust Z, but I just met him, and it's his team we're investigating. He might not be too happy about throwing his own teammates and coach under the bus. Are you sure you don't mind?"

"Mind?" Bess spluttered. "Are you kidding? I live for this stuff! Let me look at their schedule and see which classes they have tonight." She gulped the rest of her coffee and started poking at her phone.

George leaned over to me and muttered, "Whatever happened to Bess 'If It Messes Up My Hair, I Don't Want to Do It' Marvin?"

"I don't know," I replied, "but this new Bess certainly is entertaining!" I opened my closet and pulled out some clothes for the day. "In the meantime, George, I'd like you to help me out with something. I want to follow up on that locker break-in. I still think the perpetrator probably meant to break into Carly's locker . . . but I have to be sure that there's no chance Penny is involved somehow. I have no idea how she could be connected to all of this, but I don't like loose ends. I'll call Libby at Iron Dragon and see if she knows where Penny might be this morning."

George nodded. "Good thinking. Happy to tag along."

"Can you guys drop me off downtown?" Bess asked as I finished getting dressed. "I need to do a little shopping."

"No problem!" I said. The coffee and the thought of forging ahead with the investigation had blown the last traces of sleep from my mind. Sure, my body still felt like it had been hit by a pickup truck, but there's no better medicine than a mystery. . . .

An hour later, after grabbing some breakfast and dropping off Bess, George and I drove to the outskirts of town. We searched among the maze of warehouses, using the directions Libby had given us. Apparently, Penny's last name was Forrester, and she worked with a construction company during the week, so we would hopefully be able to find her there.

"So, did you discover anything interesting from your Jiu-Jitsu research?" I asked George as we drove.

She nodded. "Lots, actually. There are five belts in Jiu-Jitsu: white, blue, purple, brown, and black. And they don't come easy. It takes most people about ten years to earn a black belt."

"Wow," I said. "That's quite a commitment."

"Yeah, that seems to be a big part of it. From what I read, the good schools don't just promote people based on whether they can defeat everyone in the room. They also judge students on their character. If the student helps make the whole academy better, then they're considered more seriously for a promotion to the next belt."

I thought about Liam and the way he'd reacted when I'd asked about his purple belt, and how long he'd been doing Jiu-Jitsu. Maybe he'd expected to be a black belt by now and felt embarrassed that he wasn't. *It must be hard to feel like you've fallen behind your own expectations for yourself,* I thought. I knew that there had been cases in the past—tough cases—where I felt like I'd missed obvious clues and let important information slip past me. I'd been an amateur detective for a long time, and like Liam, I guess I had pretty high expectations for myself too.

"There it is!" George said, pointing to a sign up ahead, posted on the side of a small building inside a fenced area filled with construction vehicles and equipment. The words TRIANGLE CONSTRUCTION were printed in black on a large red triangle.

"Bingo," I said, and steered my car into a small parking lot nearby. Half a dozen cars, including a dingy-looking white hatchback with a blue air freshener hanging from the rearview mirror, were already parked in the lot. I recognized the hatchback as the same one I'd seen parked in front of Iron Dragon. "Penny must be here. I'm pretty sure that's her car."

A half dozen construction workers were carrying materials out of a truck and checking equipment when George and I walked up to the trailer that housed the company offices. A man who must have been the supervisor stepped out of it and approached us. He wore a white hard hat and sported a thick mustache. "Can I help you?" he asked.

"Yes," I replied. "We're Penny Forrester's friends. We couldn't get ahold of her over the phone, so we're just wondering if we could talk to her for a second?"

The supervisor tapped a finger on his clipboard, his eyes darting back and forth between me and George. "Fine," he finally said. "But make it quick. And while you're here, you have to wear these." He ducked back into the trailer and emerged with two more white hard hats, then handed one to each of us. "She's over there," he said, and pointed across the way to where the new materials were being piled up.

"We won't keep her long, promise!" I said, plopping the hat onto my head.

As we crossed the yard, I heard a quiet, familiar melody. "Take Me Out to the Ball Game." Following the tune, I spied Penny behind a pile of lumber. She wore jeans and a black polo shirt, and her wavy brown hair was tied up in a ponytail under her hard hat. She hummed as she made notations on the clipboard in her hand.

"I need to play this cool," I murmured to George. "Only tell her what she needs to know. If she *is* somehow connected to this, I don't want to scare her."

"Got it," George said with a wink. "I'll be cool as a cucumber."

"Penny! Hello!" I called as we got closer. "It's Nancy and George from Iron Dragon. Remember us?"

From her surprised expression, *we* might as well have been dragons. "Oh! What, uh, what are you guys doing here?"

"I know this probably isn't the best time," I said.

"But I'm still investigating what's been going on at Iron Dragon, so this really couldn't wait. Did you happen to hear about the fire at the academy last night?"

Penny nodded. "Everyone was texting about it this morning. Why?"

"Well, it's the strangest thing," I said. "Coach Ethan told me that whoever set the fire also broke into one of the lockers. Your locker, actually. I hope you didn't have anything valuable in there."

Penny's face went pale. "No, no," she said after a moment. "Nothing valuable at all—just a spare gi and some athletic tape, a notebook . . . Didn't anyone else's lockers get broken into?"

"See, that's the funny thing," I replied. "It was only yours."

"Oh," Penny said, swallowing hard. "That's weird."

"We can't imagine why anyone would go to the trouble of breaking a padlock just to get into your locker," I said. "Can you?"

"No," said Penny. "I can't." She squeezed the pen in her hand, clicking and unclicking it as she spoke. "Look, I'm pretty new here. I've only been in River Heights for about six months. I was raised in New York and moved here when this job opened up. I didn't know anybody, so I thought it would be fun to start training at Iron Dragon. Make some friends, you know? I haven't had time to get wrapped up in anything crazy. Didn't I hear that you thought this whole thing was about Carly and the tournament on Saturday? I mean, I'm not even a competitor. Doesn't that make a lot more sense than someone coming after me?"

"Yeah," I admitted. "It does."

Her hunch mirrored my own—that her locker being broken into was probably an accident. Everything seemed to lead back to Carly, which left me with lots of theories, but not one bit of proof.

"I'm sorry you came all this way for nothing," Penny said, still clicking her pen. "But I really should get back to work now."

I sighed and nodded. "Of course. Sorry to bother you."

My mood was grim as George and I got back into the car. I started the ignition and caught Penny's supervisor watching us in the rearview mirror.

"Sheesh," George said, chuckling. "It's like he's afraid we're going to run off with a bulldozer or something."

I didn't reply. Putting the car into gear, I steered us back toward town.

George cleared her throat and pulled out her phone. "Well, um, I'll text Bess and tell her we're heading back. She should be done by now." After a minute of silence, George looked over at me. "C'mon, Nancy, buck up! I know it's disappointing that we don't have much to go on yet, but we'll figure this out. We always do."

I shook my head. "I know, but I'm missing something, I can feel it."

"Maybe," said George. "Hmm. What is it they say about returning to the scene of the crime? Maybe that's what we need to do."

I thought about that for a moment and nodded. "You might be right. If Bess is going to be our spy over at Lockdown, the best thing for us to do is keep watch over at Iron Dragon and wait for the perpetrator to make their next move. They've already hit the academy twice, and the tournament is only two days away. If Carly is still planning on fighting, then there's a good chance they'll try again. And we need to be there to catch them in the act." I felt my heart lift a little now that I had a plan going forward. "Thanks, George," I said. "That's just what I needed."

She looked a little surprised, then shrugged and laced her fingers behind her head. "It was nothing. Just routine detective work."

I grinned and pulled up to the curb, where Bess was waiting for us in front of a row of stores. She was carrying a large plastic shopping bag and wearing a dazzling smile. "Look what I bought!" she exclaimed as she slid into the back seat. George and I turned to see her pull a brand-new white Jiu-Jitsu gi from the bag. It had vines of pink flowers stitched across the shoulders and down the lapels. "Isn't it beautiful?" Bess said, hugging it to her chest.

George and I gave each other a look. "Ho boy," George mumbled. "She's got it bad!"

CHAPTER EIGHT

Human Chess

THAT NIGHT, WHILE BESS AND HER NEW GI went to do some method acting at Lockdown, George and I steeled ourselves for another class at Iron Dragon. I really thought that after nearly being mugged, half a dozen rounds of sparring with as many people, a midnight chase, and nearly being burned to a crisp, my body would finally say, *Enough is enough*. But like Chef Kathy said that night in the soup kitchen, *You do the impossible often enough, it becomes routine*. Somehow, I wasn't broken, so off I went for more Jiu-Jitsu.

I feared the academy might have to close for a

while, but the police finished examining the scene and allowed classes to resume. When we walked into the lobby, the hallway where the fire had been was cordoned off. The walls, ceiling, and floor were completely blackened. The air was still slightly smoky, though someone had tried to mask the smell with a pine-scented air freshener.

Libby was sitting behind her desk, and her eyes lit up when she saw us. "Nancy!" she said. "I heard what happened last night! Are you all right?"

I nodded. "Totally fine. I'm just glad everything turned out okay. I'm guessing Carly heard too. How's she holding up?"

Libby's face fell. "Not great. She thinks that she's responsible for all of this, and that whoever's targeting her won't stop until she drops out of the tournament."

George shook her head. "But we don't know that for sure yet. And even if this is about her, she can't let them win!"

Libby shrugged. "I know. That's what Coach Ethan told her too. But it seems like she's made up her mind. Maybe you should talk to her, Nancy."

"Yeah, maybe I should."

As George and I made our way to the training room, another group was just finishing up a kickboxing class. Jeremy, the big blue belt, was hitting one of the hanging punching bags with savage jabs. The bag was swinging so wildly, it almost hit another student in the face. Jeremy stopped and steadied the bag. He caught us watching from across the room and grinned. "I don't know, ladies. Either I'm getting stronger, or this bag is getting lighter."

I chuckled and called out, "My bet's on the first one!"

"I think we've reached the point in the night when I pray for my survival," George mumbled.

"Don't you think you're being a little dramatic?" I asked.

Just then Jeremy wound up for a cross, connecting with the punching bag so hard that it almost sailed right off its chain.

George went pale. I patted her on the shoulder. "You'll be fine," I said, hoping I sounded more confident than I felt. "Just keep your eyes and ears open for anything that might be useful."

As we walked toward the women's locker room to get changed, Liam emerged from the men's locker room. He smiled when he saw me.

"Well," I said, glancing at the purplish welt on his forehead. "I'm surprised to see you back in class so soon."

Liam waved a hand at me. "Oh, it's just a little bump. No reason to keep me off the mats."

"You're like the post office!" George joked as she put her hand over her heart. "Neither snow nor rain nor heat nor minor concussions will keep me away from wrestling with my friends."

Liam laughed. "Yup, that's pretty much it." A moment later Penny came through the lobby toward us. Liam excused himself and walked over to her. "You still good for our private lesson tomorrow night? Let's say nine?"

"I'll be there," Penny replied. She glanced over my way, and I nodded in greeting.

"You coming?" George asked me, gesturing toward the locker room.

"Sure," I said, and followed her in. We found Carly standing by the lockers, slowly tying her purple belt around her waist. "Hey," I said, setting down my bag.

"Hey," Carly replied, not meeting my eyes.

"Listen," I began, keeping my voice soft. "I know how you must be feeling about everything, but please don't pull out of the tournament. We're going to figure this out, and—"

Carly looked up at me, her brown eyes full of anguish. "Nancy," she said, cutting me off. "Whoever's threatening me almost burned the whole building down! Liam could have *died*!"

"But Carly," I pleaded, "we don't know for sure yet that this is even about you."

"What else could it be about?" she asked.

I opened my mouth, but no words came out. Frustration welled up in my chest. This case seemed so clear-cut—so why wasn't anything adding up?

Seeing the doubt in my eyes, Carly shook her head. "I thought so." She sighed. "I can't believe that Lucy would be behind something like this. Brock, maybe, but it just seems so awful. They must really hate me. Anyway, if I drop out now, maybe they'll leave us alone—"

"No," George piped up. "You can't give up. Coach Ethan doesn't want you to, and I'm willing to bet the rest of the team doesn't want you to either. You guys are all fighters—are you really going to let someone intimidate you like this?"

Carly sank onto a bench and dropped her head into her hands. "I don't know. I don't know what to do."

"Just, please—give me a little more time," I told her.

After a few tense moments, Carly nodded. "All right, I trust you, Nancy. Just don't make me regret it. If I have to drop out at the last minute, I will."

"I won't let you down," I said.

She got up and left the locker room, and George and I started putting on our own gis. A sick feeling filled my stomach as I tied my white belt. *She trusts me, but I'm not so sure I trust myself.*

Once we were dressed, George and I walked to the training room to bow in. With the big tournament only two days away, all the competitors were putting in one last big push to get ready. Everyone was panting and dripping with sweat after the grueling warm-up—I must have guzzled half my water bottle by the time we were done.

"Ugh, why is there sand on the mat?" George muttered, brushing off her feet.

Jamie was standing next to us, and she bent her knee to inspect the bottoms of her own feet. "Huh," she said, and brushed hers off too. "Someone must have tracked it in from outside. Probably all those firefighters and policemen who were in here."

I wiped the sweat from my brow and peered at the thermostat on the wall. Despite the fact that it was warm outside, for some reason, Coach Ethan had turned up the heat to eighty degrees.

"Why does it have to be so hot in here?" I groaned.

Jamie shrugged. "Competing is really stressful," she whispered back. "On the mind and on the body. If you get used to it being hard here in the room, it makes the competition a little bit easier. There's a quote Coach always tells us: 'Under pressure, you don't rise to the occasion, you sink to the level of your training. That's why we train hard.' You know what I mean?"

I thought about that idea, then nodded. It was true that during those times when I was in real danger, my mind went on autopilot. If I didn't have all that experience dealing with sticky situations, I probably would lose control and panic. You can't expect to survive a fire if you aren't used to taking the heat.

After our water break, all the students sat in a circle around Coach Ethan and Nate, a purple belt who he'd called out to help demonstrate the evening's technique. "In many ways," Coach Ethan said as the lesson began, "Jiu-Jitsu is like human chess. For every move you make"—he reached out to grab the lapel of Nate's gi—"there's a move your opponent can make to defend against it." In response, Nate grabbed Coach Ethan's outstretched arm and dragged it forward so that he could swing around to the head coach's back. From there, he grabbed Coach Ethan around the waist and drove him down to the mat.

"You see?" Coach Ethan said, rising to a kneeling position once Nate had released his grip. "I made my move, Nate made his. And like I always say, what's the first rule of Jiu-Jitsu? If you can do it . . ."

"Attack the back!" the class finished.

"That's right," Coach Ethan said. "So, if every move has a countermove, you need a strategy, just like a chess player. You need to know all the different ways that your opponent could react, so you're always two steps ahead." He and Nate got back up and reset their position. "Sometimes you can take advantage of what your opponent thinks you're going to do and trick them into putting themselves in a bad spot." This time, when Coach Ethan reached out his hand and Nate leaned forward to grab it, the coach instantly dropped to his knee and shot forward, grabbing Nate by both legs and knocking *him* to the mat. "You can throw your opponent off-balance by faking one move to cover up what you're really planning," Coach Ethan said, getting to his feet once more and facing the class. "But remember, your opponent can do the same thing. Underestimating them could cost you the whole match. Jiu-Jitsu may look like it's only a contest of strength and agility, but it's just as much a battle of wits. If you can outsmart your opponent, you're that much closer to winning the game."

After Nate and Coach Ethan finished teaching us how to do the double leg takedown he'd shown, the class split up into pairs to drill the technique. Somehow I ended up being partnered with Jeremy. George, who was drilling with Jamie across the room, grinned wickedly my way and gave me two thumbs-up.

Jeremy must have seen the concern on my face. "Don't worry," he said, taking off his glasses and setting them aside. "Part of being good at wrecking people is also knowing how *not* to wreck people." True to his word, working on the takedowns together turned out to be a breeze. Despite being a giant, Jeremy was very light on his feet. We soon got into a regular rhythm of knocking each other over.

After a few minutes, my mind began to wander. I couldn't stop thinking about the case. How was it that all the clues pointed to Carly's past at Lockdown, yet I couldn't find any solid evidence to nail down a suspect? Why couldn't I shake the feeling that something about this mystery was very, very wrong?

With all these thoughts filling my head, I wasn't ready when Jeremy came in for the next takedown. His shoulders hit me in the belly, knocking me back to my senses—but not fast enough. An instant later, my body hit the ground like a sack of bricks.

Wham!

I lay gasping on the mat. *Well,* I thought, *that's what you get for not paying attention.*

"Hey, are you okay?" Jeremy asked. "You didn't break your fall."

"Yeah," I said, sitting up with a grimace. "It was my fault. I was distracted."

"Something on your mind?"

"You could say that."

"School stuff? Home stuff?"

"Mystery-solving stuff, actually."

"Ohhh," Jeremy said, his eyes lighting up. "So

do you know who marked up our academy and set it on fire?"

"Not yet," I admitted. "But something that Coach Ethan said earlier stuck with me. The whole part about faking one move to cover up the real plan . . ."

Jeremy studied me with interest. "Is someone trying to throw you off-balance, Nancy?"

"I don't know. But I'm going to find out."

A couple of hours later, George and I were sitting at my kitchen table at home, scarfing down take-out cartons of lo mein that we'd picked up on the way home. Despite all our worrying, we'd both had a really good time in class, and even though I was starving and exhausted, for the first time since this case started, I felt like I was thinking clearly.

"Anything left for me?" Bess asked, coming in the back door and dropping her gym bag on the floor.

George, her mouth crammed with noodles, pushed the carton of lo mein across the table to her cousin.

"You guys are the best," said Bess. She opened

the carton and blissfully inhaled the cloud of Chinese food smells that wafted out before tucking in with her chopsticks.

"Anything to report?" I asked her.

Bess shook her head. "Unfortunately, no. Master Brock obviously has a chip on his shoulder about the Carly thing—I overheard him and Lucy Hayes talking about the tournament and strategizing about how to beat her. But no suspicious whispering about threats or mischief at Iron Dragon. And nothing that points to them having hired help to terrorize the competition. Maybe the evidence is there, but I couldn't find it. Sorry, Nancy."

"Don't apologize. Sometimes *not* finding any evidence is evidence in itself. If anything, it makes me think that my new theory might be right after all."

"What new theory?" Bess asked.

"That I've been barking up the wrong tree."

George popped a shrimp into her mouth. "What do you mean?"

"From the very beginning of this case, I assumed

that Carly was the target. I mean, why wouldn't I? It made sense, and there was no reason for me to doubt it. But what if someone was putting those clues there to throw me off? What if, by following all those fake clues, I ended up ignoring the real ones?"

"You're thinking about Penny, aren't you?" George asked.

I nodded. "Something about the way she acted at the construction site, and tonight, was weird. She seemed nervous, awkward—like she's hiding something. The only question is: What?"

George set down her chopsticks. "Where's your laptop?" she asked.

"It's in my bag by the door," I answered. "Why?"

She got up to grab it. "Because," she said, setting up the computer on the table and cracking her knuckles, "whatever Penny might be hiding, the magic of the Internet shall reveal."

George opened up a search window and typed in Penny's name. While Bess and I finished our late-night meal, George clicked away, her brows furrowed in concentration as she stared at the screen. I was polishing off the last bite of an egg roll when she sat back in her chair with a "Huh."

"What is it?" I asked. "What did you find?"

"Nothing," George said. "Well, almost nothing. That's the weird thing. Penny said she lived in New York before moving to River Heights, but there's no record of her anywhere in the state. Nothing on public record or on social media that matches her description. It's almost like Penny Forrester didn't exist before six months ago, when she moved to town."

"Maybe she didn't," I said, rubbing my chin. "What if Penny Forrester is a false identity? Maybe she didn't move to River Heights for a job. Could she have come here to get away from something?"

"Or some*one*," Bess added.

"Right," I said, getting up and pacing the room. "That would explain why she was being so evasive when we started asking questions. If *she's* the target of the threats, she might be more interested in protecting her true identity than helping us stop whoever is after her." This new information filled me with a burst of fresh energy. Finally my gut was telling me we were on the right track. "So, let's say our hunch is correct. Without knowing anything about Penny's past, we're still looking at a whole lot of nothing. Who's coming after her, and why?"

The question hung in the air. I needed to do something with my hands, so I started to gather up all the empty cartons and other bits of trash from the table. I grabbed a packet of soy sauce, not realizing it was open, and it squirted a pool of brown liquid all over some of Dad's documents that we'd shoved off to the side before we started chowing down. "Shoot!" I exclaimed, and quickly grabbed some napkins to mop it up. As I was wiping the papers, something on one of the reports caught my eye—the words *Crazy Eights*.

My breath caught in my throat. I picked up the document and quickly read through it, my pulse quickening. Once I was done, I picked up my gym bag and started rummaging through it, throwing my sweaty gi and workout clothes onto the floor.

"I can't believe it!" I muttered under my breath. "It was right in front of my face all this time!"

"Nancy . . . ," Bess said slowly, the way you'd talk to a spooked animal. "What are you doing? What was on that paper?"

Finally I found my phone and pulled up the photo I'd snapped of the matchbox. "When I was chasing that person through the alley, this fell out of their pocket," I said, turning the screen so Bess and George could see. "I couldn't see how it had anything to do with the case at the time, but look at this report from my dad's case files. He was gathering documents about a series of bank robberies from a few years ago. The last one was in Rosedale—the robbery of Viana Bank. The robbers were caught; Dad prosecuted the case that sent them to prison. This report says that as part of the investigation, they interviewed people from both Viana Bank and from the pub next door: Crazy Eights. Apparently, someone who was working at Crazy Eights was involved in the robbery."

"Okay, so our arsonist got their matches from a

pub in Rosedale," George said, puzzled. "Why is that important?"

"It's important because of what's next door to Iron Dragon MMA," I explained.

Bess's jaw dropped. "A bank."

"Wait. If the robberies happened a few years ago, and the criminals are in jail, why's your dad digging up the case again?"

"Good question," I said in a low voice. "Because the robbers escaped."

"When?" George asked, but I think she already knew the answer.

"About a week ago."

Bess, George, and I exchanged glances as the pieces began to fall into place. "Maybe this case isn't about Jiu-Jitsu at all," I said. "Maybe it's actually about the same thing as most other crimes: money. So we've got Penny, who seems to be the victim of these threats, and a connection to two escaped bank robbers. But how do they fit together?" I picked up some other papers from the table, studying each one in turn. "It looks like Dad

~ 126 ~

must have already taken most of the documents to the police. Nothing here has any information that seems useful."

A moment later, as if he knew I was thinking about him, Dad shuffled into the kitchen. He tied the rope of his bathrobe around his waist and yawned. "Don't you girls ever *sleep*?" he asked.

"Dad," I said excitedly, "I think there's a connection between your old case and my new one."

Dad's eyes brightened as I quickly caught him up on what we'd discovered. "Fascinating," he said, plopping down on one of the kitchen chairs. "It's a long shot, but there might be something there."

"Is there anything else you remember about the case? Any more details?" I asked.

Dad rubbed his chin, thinking. "Hmm, it's been a few years and a few hundred cases since I worked on this one, honey," he admitted. "And I didn't look at the files when I pulled them. I just put them in a box and delivered what I thought was pertinent to the case. I'm sorry, Nance."

I blew out the air from my cheeks. "It's okay. We'll find another way."

Suddenly Dad snapped his fingers. "Wait a minute," he said. "There was a reporter from the *Bugle* who was covering the case back then. It was a big story at the time, and she wrote a lot of detailed coverage about the robberies. I bet if you got your hands on those old articles, they'd give you all the information you need."

I grinned. *Now we're getting somewhere!* I ran over to give him a big hug. "Thanks, Dad! You're the best."

"I'm even better after a full night's sleep," he grumbled, but I could feel him smiling against my shoulder. "Now," he said, rubbing his eyes, "will you girls *please* leave the rest of the mystery solving for tomorrow?"

We all agreed, and Dad bid us good night and clomped back upstairs to bed.

As George rose from her chair, I grabbed her wrist. "Before you go, can you do a quick check for those articles online?"

"No problem," she replied, and quickly went to work finding the *River Heights Bugle* website and searching their digital archives. After a few minutes, she sighed and shook her head in frustration. "No luck. It looks like the public archives only cover a twenty-four-month timespan—and those robberies happened three years ago."

"Ugh, how annoying," Bess said.

"Wait a minute." A new idea had popped into my head. "It's the *Bugle*. . . ."

George nodded. "Yeah, why?"

I grinned. "Because a big fan of mine just happens to work there." I pulled out my phone and sent a quick text.

Ever since this case started, I hadn't been able to shake that feeling that I was being manipulated, fighting a losing game. Well, it was time for that to change. Tomorrow I was going to pay a visit to the *Bugle* offices to see my new friend Z. And I was finally going to get some answers.

CHAPTER NINE

~

Getting the Hooks In

THE NEXT DAY DAWNED WITH MOUNTAINS of clouds rolling in over River Heights, bringing wind and the promise of rain. Z couldn't see me until he was done with work, so I spent the day running errands around town. Since Hannah was still away, I thought it would be nice to take care of some things so she wouldn't have as much to do when she got back. After taking a couple of packages to the post office, picking up the dry cleaning and some groceries, and grabbing a bite to eat at the deli down the street, I finally got back home, weighed down with grocery bags and questions. Despite keeping myself busy throughout the day, I hadn't been able to stop thinking about the case. The end was closing in—I could feel it as strongly as the oncoming storm.

After putting all the stuff away, I checked the time on my phone and realized I was supposed to meet Z in fifteen minutes! *Man,* I thought, *I almost killed too much time!*

I jumped back into the car, drove downtown for the second time that day, and parked in front of the *Bugle* offices. They were in an old building with arched windows, and its weathered redbrick and stone facade looked like it had seen better days. It was five o'clock, so workers were streaming out of the doors, making me feel like a salmon swimming upstream as I tried to get inside. When I finally reached the front office, the administrative assistant was putting on her coat to leave.

"Zhuang?" she repeated when I explained to her who I was there to see. "Oh right. He said he was expecting someone. He's back in the archive room—down the hall, fifth door on the left."

I thanked her and walked past a newsroom, the art department, and editors' offices until I reached a door marked HERALD ARCHIVES. Inside, boxes were crammed onto shelves and piled up on the floor. At least a dozen ancient computers added to the clutter, their yellowed keyboards sticking haphazardly out of a wide box like some kind of bizarre flower bouquet.

The air was alive with dust motes, and the moment I stepped inside, I started to cough. My lungs still hadn't quite recovered from all the smoke. "Z, are you in here?" I croaked. "It's Nancy."

Z's head popped out from behind one of the tall shelves. "Oh, hey!" he said with a wide smile. "How goes the mystery solving, dude?"

"It goes okay," I said. "It's been a rough couple of days." Walking toward him, I saw that Z was standing by a table covered with old issues of the *Bugle*. After pulling up a chair, I sat down and caught him up on everything that had happened since we'd met on Wednesday night.

Z's eyebrows climbed farther and farther up his

forehead as the story unfolded. "Dang, dude," he said once I was done. "You want a Coke or something?"

I grinned. "Actually, a Coke sounds great."

Z left the room and came back with two ice-cold cans of soda. He popped his open and took a swig. "So," he said. "I pulled a bunch of those old papers you asked for. Check it out."

I took a closer look at the newspapers on the table and realized that each was turned to an article about the bank robberies. "All of these are for me?" I asked, amazed.

"Well, yeah," he replied. "When Nancy Drew asks you to help her with a case, you don't do it halfway."

"Z, this is fantastic!" I said, beaming. *Looks like your trust in him paid off,* I thought.

"Everything is in chronological order," Z went on, pointing. "Articles about the first robbery are over here, and they go all the way to the arrests and jail sentences for the two bank robbers over there. I could have looked up the files on our computer network, but I thought you'd prefer being able to see them all laid out together. Like they do in cop movies. It's easier to see everything at once, isn't it?"

"Absolutely," I said.

"So, what do these old robberies have to do with your Jiu-Jitsu crime?" Z asked.

"That's kind of what I'm trying to figure out. I'm wondering if the person who's been threatening someone at Iron Dragon might be one of the escaped bank robbers from this case. When I was chasing a suspect out of the academy the other night, a matchbook fell out of their pocket—a matchbook from the same place that was used to break into a bank next door to it a few years ago. Iron Dragon is next to a bank too—could there be a connection? And then there's this girl at Iron Dragon—Penny Forrester. We think she might actually be the target of the threats. She might even be hiding in River Heights under a false identity, but I don't know why. I swear it's all connected somehow. . . ."

"Like, you have a bunch of pieces of the puzzle, but you can't figure out how they fit together?" Z asked.

"Exactly right," I agreed.

Z rubbed his chin. "I get it, Nancy. Well, hopefully all this stuff will help."

I nodded, and we settled in with our Cokes to read through all the articles one at a time.

The warm light of dusk streaming through the archive's windows had faded to night by the time I'd made it through most of the newspapers. Z dug out a couple of old green-shaded lamps from some boxes and plugged them in, illuminating the tables where we sat reading.

I felt like I had a better grasp on the story behind the robberies. The basic gist was this: one night, about four years before, a bank on the edge of River Heights was robbed. The strange thing was there were no visible signs of a break-in, just an empty vault. It seemed like an inside job, but the bank's staff was very small, and all of them had alibis for that evening. Without any video evidence, the police had had no choice but to leave the case unsolved.

That is, until six months later, when a slightly larger bank in south River Heights was also robbed. Just like the first robbery, the crime happened overnight, and there didn't seem to be any obvious signs of a break-in there, either. But this time the bank had cameras, and they managed to catch a glimpse of three robbers cleaning out the vault. They were all masked, but after examining the tape, the police concluded that the thieves were two men and a woman.

While investigating the crime scene thoroughly, the police discovered a passageway that had been dug between the bank and the basement of the café next door, and then hidden afterward. When the owner of the café was interviewed, she mentioned that one of her employees who worked the late shift and closed up for her—a blond girl named Olivia Woods—had stopped showing up for work right after the robbery. After that, the police saw a connection in the crimes; there had been a girl who'd worked at the fashion boutique next door to the first bank that had been robbed.

She, too, stopped coming to work the day after the crime and couldn't be reached for comment. And once they rechecked the first bank, they were able to find another hidden passageway dug between the fashion boutique and the bank vault.

"So after the second robbery, the police were able to establish a pattern," I said, thinking out loud. "The female robber would get a job at a business next door to a bank to stake it out and gain access. Slowly, over several months, the robbers would then dig a tunnel between one building and the other. Once they broke through, they'd take whatever they could carry from the vault and disappear overnight."

The third and final bank robbery, the one at Viana Bank in Rosedale, took place about three years ago. The two male robbers were caught at the scene, thanks to an anonymous tip the police received about the planned heist. But the woman somehow eluded capture.

"Is that your dad?" Z asked, pointing to a picture in another paper of the robbers walking into the courthouse, surrounded by a bunch of lawyers.

"That's him," I said. In the photo, Dad was wearing a smart navy suit, and his face was locked in a determined gaze. "This last article says he got the accused criminals, Max and Ollie Ladrao, sentenced to twenty years in prison for robbery and breaking and entering, as well as for some previous misdemeanors."

And now the robbers were free, and were possibly the same people making trouble at Iron Dragon MMA. Were they planning another robbery, this time from the Heights Bank? But if that was the case, why were they going out of their way to threaten Penny? What did she have to do with any of this?

I drummed on the table with my fingers, thinking. "They got these two guys. But there were *three* robbers. What happened to the woman who worked in the shops next to the banks?"

I scanned the last few articles again. The only reference I could find to the third robber was that she'd never been captured, and that a small portion of the money taken from the Viana Bank vault hadn't been recovered. Max and Ollie refused to give up any information about their partner in crime and had insisted that even if they did, the police wouldn't be able to find her. She was a ghost.

And then a section of an article about the last robbery caught my eye. The headline read: COPS AND ROBBERS: BROTHERS' CRIME SPREE FINALLY COMES TO AN END.

Last night River Heights law enforcement apprehended the criminals responsible for a string of bank robberies throughout the River Heights area. Two brothers from out of state, Max and Ollie Ladrao, were captured by the RHPD in the middle of their third robbery attempt, at Viana Bank in Rosedale. All three crimes were perpetrated using a scheme that took advantage of businesses located next door to the banks.

Although there were few leads after the first two robberies, the tide turned when the police received an anonymous tip yesterday afternoon, informing them of the planned heist at Viana Bank. The two robbers were caught at the scene at eleven p.m. last night emerging from the Crazy Eights pub next door.

Police are still on the lookout for a third robber implicated in these crimes—thought to be a white woman in her early twenties. The woman is believed to be the individual who took jobs in the businesses next door to the banks to gain access to the bank vaults. However, detailed descriptions of the woman have been varied, as she is believed to be living under false identities. One of her former employers described her as "blond and blue-eyed," while another said she was "one of those goth girls with black hair and a lot of eyeliner." As for the two brothers in crime, their arraignment is set to begin this week.

"'False identities,'" I murmured. The pieces were starting to fit together now. "I think," I said slowly, "I think I've got it. But I have to be sure."

"Oh man," Z said, rubbing his hands together. "This is getting good!"

I pulled out my phone and looked up the number for the Crazy Eights pub. The phone rang a few times before someone picked up. "Crazy Eights," said a gravelly male voice. "Whaddya need?"

"Good evening, sir," I said, trying to sound official. "Are you the owner of this establishment?"

"Who wants to know?"

"My name is Nancy Drew. I'm investigating the robbery of the Viana Bank and I was wondering if I could ask you a question."

"You a cop or somethin'?"

I paused. "Something . . . like that," I said, and cleared my throat. "So, about Viana Bank?"

"That robbery? *Pshh*. That was years ago. Ancient history. Nothin' more to say about it."

"I realize that, sir. Just one question, and I won't

bother you again." When there was no response, I added, "It's extremely important."

The man grunted. "Fine, make it quick. I've got drinks to pour and dinner to serve."

I took a deep breath. "There was a young woman who worked for you at the time, right? One who disappeared after the robbery?"

"Yeah, same as those other robberies. Pretty girl—redhead with glasses, if I'm rememberin' right. Can't quite remember the name—"

"No worries," I said. "I'm just wondering . . . it's a bit of a silly question, but did she have a habit of humming while she worked?"

There was a pause. I could hear glasses clinking and people talking in the background. Then, "Actually, now that you mention it, she did. She always used to hum to herself when she was washing dishes and putting up the chairs at the end of the night. 'Take Me Out to the Ball Game,' I think it was. Why? What's so important about that?"

"Thank you, sir. Thank you very much!" I said

before hanging up the phone. My heart was pounding. I turned to Z and grabbed him by the shoulders. "I had everything all wrong. Again. Penny isn't just the target of this crime, she's *one of the criminals*! That's why she's been hiding behind a false identity. Because Penny's the missing third robber!"

"Whoa!" Z said, his dark eyes wide. "So what are you going to do now?"

My mind was racing. Three years ago, Penny Forrester—or whatever her name was—and Max and Ollie Ladrao were all partners in crime. Max and Ollie got caught at the Viana Bank heist because of an anonymous tip, but Penny got away. Then, a week ago, the brothers escaped and seemed to have been threatening Penny ever since. But why? What did they want?

One thing was for sure: if Penny had joined Iron Dragon so she could rob the Heights Bank next door, following the pattern of the other robberies, tonight would be the perfect time to do it. With the academy closed for the day and the tournament in the morning, there'd be no one there for a long time—no one to see her stealing all that money before she disappeared again, tossing "Penny Forrester" aside to assume yet another new identity.

Suddenly I remembered something else I'd overheard the night before at the academy. It had seemed so innocent at the time, but recalling it now made my blood run cold:

You still good for our private lesson tomorrow night? Let's say nine? Liam had asked.

And Penny had replied, *I'll be there!*

I looked at my phone. The clock read 8:55 p.m.

"Z, thank you so, so much for everything you did," I said, running out the door. "I have to get to Iron Dragon right now—but I'll be in touch!"

"Nancy, wait!" Z called out.

But there was no time. Liam was about to meet up with Penny at Iron Dragon—alone. She must have been using him to get into the building after hours. If she was planning to rob the bank tonight and Liam caught wind of it, who knew what she might do to him? He'd already been caught in the cross fire of this case once and gotten hurt in the process. I couldn't let it happen again!

CHAPTER TEN

~

Caught in a Choke Hold

C'MON, C'MON—I DON'T HAVE TIME TO waste!

I waited for the traffic light to change, drumming my fingers on the steering wheel in frustration. I must have hit every single red light between the *River Heights Bugle* office and Iron Dragon. After finally pulling into a parking spot in front of the academy, I picked up my phone to send a quick text to Bess and George.

it's Penny, I wrote, my thumbs flying across the screen. She's the third bank robber! And she's meeting Liam tonight. I hit send and was just starting to type out another one saying that I'd gone to Iron Dragon to warn him—when my phone went black.

"No," I whispered, tapping at the screen and pressing the power button over and over. "No-no-no-no! Not now!" But it was no use.

My phone was dead.

I should have realized I hadn't charged it all day— that it would be dangerously low after the many hours of shopping and errands and sleuthing—but I had been so preoccupied with everything that I hadn't even noticed the warnings or the red sliver on the battery bar. And now it was too late. I went to reach for my bag, which I thought had a charger inside, only to find that in my rush, I'd left it behind at the *Bugle*.

Ugh!

That must have been why Z was calling after me. . . . What else can possibly go wrong tonight?

Had the text I'd sent to Bess and George even been delivered? I knew it was a bad idea to go into a potentially dangerous situation without backup on the way, but I had no charger, and every shop on the street was already closed for the night. I dropped the useless phone on the passenger seat. If my friends *did* get the message, they should be able to figure out where I was. And if they knew I was going to Iron Dragon, they'd send help.

I bit my lip. It was a lot of ifs.

I scanned the road, searching for Penny's dingy white hatchback, but I didn't see it parked anywhere nearby. She must not have arrived yet. I looked at my car's clock: 9:02 p.m. I needed to get to Liam before she showed up and explain what was going on. If Penny tried anything, I'd feel a lot more confident with purple-belt Liam by my side.

Maybe it was a little dangerous, but I had no choice. I needed to go in now, or I risked letting Penny get away. *Again*.

I'd promised Coach Ethan that I'd solve this case, and that was exactly what I was going to do.

I climbed out of the car and took a deep breath, observing the light shining from the Iron Dragon lobby through the picture window. *Good. Liam must be here,* I thought. I popped the trunk and reached for my trusty wrench—just in case. The heavy, cool weight was reassuring in my hand. I walked to the front door, which had been taped up with cardboard since I'd broken the glass during the fire. I carefully pushed the broken door open to slip inside. The lobby was empty, but sounds of movement seemed to be coming from the coach's office.

"Liam?" I called out as I approached. "It's me, Nancy. Listen, I have to talk to you. It's about Penny—"

As I got to the door, I stopped dead. It wasn't Liam I saw standing behind the desk.

"Oh really?" said Penny. "What about me, Nancy?"

"I thought—I—" My heart leaped into my throat, silencing the rest of my words.

Penny watched me, her eyes narrowing. She was wearing black jeans, a gray Iron Dragon MMA T-shirt, and a pair of black leather gloves. "You thought what?" she asked. "You thought I wasn't here, because you didn't see my car out front? You thought that you'd sneak in and tell poor Liam that his student is really a criminal?" The warm friendliness of Jiu-Jitsu Penny, and even the guardedness of Construction Worker Penny, were gone—replaced by a cool, calculated confidence. This was the real Penny. Bank Robber Penny.

"Who are you, really?" I asked.

Penny shrugged. She picked up a red jelly bean from a dish on the desk and popped it into her mouth. "Does it matter?" she asked, chewing. "I've been so many people by now, I can hardly remember who I was when I started." She searched through the dish until she found another red jelly bean and ate that one too. "But I know who you are, Nancy Drew." She snorted and shook her head in annoyance. "Ethan hit the lottery when you walked in. You're not just a small-town girl who likes to stick her nose where it doesn't belong. No . . . you're one of River Heights's best-kept secrets. No case left unsolved. You *look* like you'd need help opening a jam jar, but looks aren't everything, are they? We both know that." She chuckled.

"So, what was it then? Your plan?" I asked, trying

to match her casual tone. She was trying to rattle me, and I wasn't going to let that happen. "You join the team here at Iron Dragon, and then once you've gained everyone's trust, you use this place to rob the bank next door? Just like you did with Max and Ollie?"

"Just like I did with Max and Ollie," Penny repeated. She sighed. "Those two were useful. For a while. I found them in some little town, just barely scraping by, shoplifting and sleeping rough, and I told them how much better they'd have it teaming up with me. I was right, of course. They were living large after that first job, but during the second hit they started getting greedy. Stopped listening. I knew that if I kept working with them, eventually we'd get caught. So when it came time for the Viana Bank job—"

"Wait," I said, realization dawning on me. "*You* called in the anonymous tip to the police, didn't you?"

Penny smiled dangerously. "What is given can just as easily be taken away."

"The word on the wall," I muttered. "'Traitor'— that's what it was about. That's why they broke out of prison and came after you. Max and Ollie found out that you were the one who turned them in."

Finally it all made sense.

"What a waste of energy," Penny said. She started to walk around the desk toward me, and I gripped the wrench in my hand more tightly. She noticed and stopped a few feet away. "You're right, of course. I thought the dead rat was overkill, but that's just me."

"But how did they find out about you ratting on them, anyway?"

"I've got a pretty good theory," Penny said. "One night I ended up telling this other lowlife I knew—a guy named Kurt—about the whole setup." She smiled at the memory. "I mean, it's a great story. Max and Ollie running from the cops on the news—you should have seen their faces! Kurt thought it was funny too, at the time. But then he got thrown in prison a couple weeks ago for pulling some dumb stunt. I'm guessing he ran into those idiots there and told them all about me being the anonymous caller. It must have burned those boys up that I turned on them like that." Penny shrugged. "Anyway, it doesn't matter much now. I'm out of here tonight with the money and getting as far from River Heights as I can. I've had it with this city."

I felt my face get hot. "Maybe it doesn't matter to you," I said, "but they've been terrorizing this academy all week! The whole place almost went up in flames, and Carly is ready to pull out of her big tournament tomorrow if it doesn't stop! I know you just joined Iron Dragon for the bank robbery, but you've been in classes with these people for months now. They've treated you as a teammate—a friend! Don't *they* matter to you at all?"

For a moment, Penny's cool expression slipped, and I saw something like regret cross her face. "Carly didn't deserve to get mixed up in this . . . but hey, you can't make an omelet without breaking a few eggs. Oh, and speaking of the job—if you don't mind, it's time for me to finish it."

Penny took another step toward me, and I moved to block her from leaving, lifting the heavy wrench to prove I meant business.

"I don't think so," I said. "Not this time." I glanced at

the cordless telephone on the desk. It was almost within arm's reach. If I could just get to it and call the police . . .

Penny's eyes followed my gaze and then darted back to the wrench. "You don't have it in you to fight me, Nancy. Why don't you just put down that thing before you hurt yourself?"

This girl certainly has a lot of nerve, I thought angrily. But I couldn't risk losing my cool now. I needed to stay calm. I took a deep breath and cast my mind back to my first sparring session with Jamie—to the way her face looked as she got ready to fight. She hadn't smiled, cocky and confident that she'd win, and she hadn't scowled, trying to frighten me into submission. Her approach was much more effective. Her face had been completely calm, a mask of total self-assurance that whatever was about to happen, she was going to be able to handle it.

That was the face I put on as I faced Penny. I straightened my back, gripped the wrench, and said evenly, "Try me."

Penny pressed her lips into a thin smile, but I could see her balling her hands into fists.

It was like Coach Ethan said: we were playing human chess, and I had just made an unexpected move. Clearly, Penny didn't like it.

I inched toward the phone, holding my weapon steady while backing Penny into the corner. The phone was nearly in my hand when I felt a shadow pass over me. Penny's eyes flicked to the door, and she smiled.

I started to turn around, but before I could, something hit me on the back of the head—hard.

A moan escaped my lips as I collapsed to the floor. Fiery pain bloomed from the base of my skull. I lay with my face against the thin, smoky-smelling carpet, just trying to breathe.

"It took you long enough," I heard Penny say over the rushing sound that filled my ears. I felt her move above me, crossing over to kick the wrench away from my hand. "I've been stuck in here with her for ten minutes. She almost called the police! What have you been doing?"

Who was she talking to? It couldn't be Max or Ollie. They'd been trying to sabotage her all along. . . .

"I was working, like you told me to," a familiar male voice replied. "Filling up all those bags takes time. Do you want me to be fast or good?"

"I want you to be both," Penny snapped. "Nancy here has it all figured out. She's a lot smarter than you gave her credit for. Your little misdirection didn't keep her off the scent for long."

The man sighed heavily. "I don't understand. It was perfect! Carly being targeted by the Lockdown guys made total sense, and the whole monkey-on-the-jacket thing was inspired, if I say so myself."

Penny huffed. "Well, unfortunately for us, it wasn't good enough to convince *her*."

And then I knew.

In my excitement at cracking the case, I'd missed one important detail. Who had been the one to encourage Carly to tell me about her past history at Lockdown? And who had given me that crucial clue from the fire, identifying the logo on the back of the attacker's jacket? I'd never considered even for a moment that he was part of this.

But if I'd learned anything about Penny's bank robberies, it was this:

She never worked alone.

I rolled over to my back, my head pounding. Penny was standing in the doorway. She passed a white belt to Liam, who was dressed in all black, his red hair loose and coated in fine gray dust. From my vantage point, he looked impossibly tall.

"Tie her up and bring her with you. I'm not risking her messing with our plans again," Penny ordered. "I'm going down to make sure you didn't miss anything, and then we're out of here. Got it? We're already running behind schedule." Then she was gone.

"Got it," Liam called after her. He turned to me, looking a little remorseful. "Sorry, Nancy. It's nothing personal, you know."

"Hitting me on the head seems really personal," I murmured.

He sighed and knelt down, turning me on my side so he could tie my hands behind my back with the belt. "Look, you don't understand what it's like around here. I've been training for nine years, and Ethan won't promote me or give me any authority. He won't even let me coach the advanced class—only *basics*. I've won the regional championship *every year* since I got my purple! But Ethan refuses to acknowledge my talent! He doesn't understand me, or how much I need this. How much I want to make this a career, not just a hobby." Once he was done, he came around in front of me again. "But after tonight, I can get out of River Heights and use this money to open up an academy of my own. No one gets hurt, and I get everything I ever wanted. You understand, don't you?"

I looked up at him. The movement made the room spin. I coughed, feeling sick. "I understand that Coach Ethan made the right choice not to promote you."

Liam's expression turned stormy, and he grabbed me by the arm, pulling me roughly to my feet. "Enough talk," he growled. "Let's go."

The noise in my head became a roar, and suddenly I felt myself falling into a darkness that swallowed me whole.

CHAPTER ELEVEN

Double Leg Takedown

THE FIRST THING TO COME BACK WAS THE pain.

My skull throbbed as I came to, a sharp, searing pain that immediately made me want to be unconscious again. There was also a strange, swinging sensation that I didn't understand right away.

Next came the voices. I could hear them as the roaring in my ears began to fade. They were muffled and far away, but as the moments passed, the voices grew louder and clearer.

"What are we going to do with her?"

"We'll put her in the trunk. Drop her somewhere on the edge of town. By the time they find her, we'll be long gone."

Liam and Penny, I thought as full consciousness returned. I opened my eyes and realized I was upside down—thrown over Liam's shoulder like a sack of potatoes—and being carried across the training room. I watched the mats pass beneath me as I tried to catch what they were saying.

"But once the police find her, she'll tell them about me," Liam said after a pause. "What about my reputation?"

"I guess you'll have to get yourself a new identity, like I did," Penny replied.

"But I—I can't do that!" Liam stammered. "People will ask about my martial arts lineage . . . where I got my belts from. What will I say? What about the new academy I was going to open?"

Peeking around Liam's back, I saw Penny shrug. "Move to Europe. That's where I'm going. They have Jiu-Jitsu there too, don't they? They'd probably ask a lot fewer questions, especially if you slip a bit of cash their way." When Liam didn't respond, Penny added, "Maybe you should have thought of that before you agreed to help me pull this heist. Like it or not, you're a criminal now—so you'd better figure it out, and fast."

Liam stopped suddenly. The reality of what he'd done must have finally crashed over him like a tidal wave.

I waited until I heard Penny's footsteps recede. "Liam," I said, my voice cracking. My throat was dry and sticky. I tried to clear it before continuing. "There's still time to do the right thing. Let me go. We can fix this."

He didn't say anything at first, but I could feel his hands shaking. And then he muttered, "I didn't know about her past, you know. Not at first."

"You didn't?" I asked, hoping to keep him talking. I needed to stall as long as I possibly could.

"I just thought she was a really attentive student. She seemed to appreciate my talent. I confided in her one day about my problems with Coach Ethan, and pretty soon she came up with this idea to rob the bank. I thought it was crazy at first, but she was so convincing. It wasn't until that night with you and the dead rat that she told me the truth. She had the idea to convince you Carly was the target, and it all just went from there. It all sort of . . . happened."

I turned my head to try to look at him. "Liam, maybe Coach Ethan hasn't promoted you yet because you really aren't ready. No amount of cash, no shiny new academy, and no belt is going to change that. Carly said that Jiu-Jitsu isn't just about the technique, it's about character. It's about who you are. The only way you're going to succeed is if you face the truth. Because the truth will find you, no matter how far you run."

A long silence followed, and I squeezed my eyes shut, hoping that my words would make Liam come to his senses.

But a few moments later, I heard staccato footsteps, loud and getting louder.

"Liam! What are you waiting for? Get down here!"

Whatever argument was going on in Liam's head

had been drowned out by Penny's harsh command. He started walking again—rapidly—toward a dark doorway I hadn't noticed before. My head bounced painfully against his back. "It's too late," he whispered. "It's much too late."

As he slipped through the doorway and down a set of metal stairs, my mind began to race. I was losing hope that my text to Bess and George had been delivered and that they were on the way. For all I knew, I was completely on my own.

I mentally went through my options. None of them looked particularly good. I could try to stall some more, hold on until someone noticed I was missing and came looking for me, but I couldn't stand the idea of just waiting around to be rescued. I didn't have much time left, anyway.

No, my best bet was to create a diversion and use that as an opportunity to try to escape. Even with my hands tied, I could run and, hopefully, find someone within a couple of blocks to help me. With the decision made, I allowed myself to be carried into the belly of the building without a struggle, waiting for my moment to strike.

As Liam reached the bottom of the stairs, I craned my head to get a good look at my surroundings. The cellar of the academy was exactly as I would have expected—concrete walls and floor, empty metal shelves, a few bare bulbs lighting the place. The only unusual things about the space were the industrial drill and tunneling auger on the floor, and the four-foot hole in the far wall, leading into darkness.

The air was thick with gray dust, which billowed up all around me when Liam set me down. "Finally," Penny said, poking her head out from the tunnel. "Just FYI, it's not a good time for second thoughts, partner. Things don't often go well for people who disappoint me on the job." She tossed a few cloth bags—surely filled with stolen cash—on the floor near my feet. I coughed as more dust went flying into the air.

"No second thoughts," Liam said, but he wouldn't meet my eyes. He picked up the cloth bags and looked inside. "I don't think we can fit these last few stacks of cash with the others, so I'll stick them in here." He picked up a black gym bag from the floor and quickly dumped the cash from the bags inside it. That done, he grabbed a bucket sitting nearby and began filling up the empty cloth bags with sand. Once they were half full, he sealed them up and brushed off his hands. "That should be it," he said. "I'll put these back in the vault now."

"Good," Penny replied with a satisfied smile. "It looks like all the bags are exactly where they're supposed to be. The bankers shouldn't notice anything amiss until they get the night deposit on Monday, and by then, we'll be long gone. An improvement on my last heist, I think."

Liam stooped to enter the tunnel. "Hurry up!" Penny shouted after him. "It's going to be a two-man job getting the cash out of here!" Once he was gone, she brushed a cloud of gray dust from her hair and pulled out her phone. Apparently, she didn't like what she saw, because she scowled and started to pace.

"Pretty lucky that Iron Dragon doesn't use this

space for storage," I said, killing time while I racked my brain to come up with a plan. "Otherwise, this heist of yours would have been hard to pull off."

"Oh, it's one of the first things I found out when I started coming to this place," she said with satisfaction. "On my first day, after scoping it out, I 'accidentally' opened this door and searched the cellar until Ethan came to find me. I played dumb and told him I thought it was the way to the bathroom. Of course he bought it. He explained to me that it was a storage room they never used. A few days later, once I started coming to classes, I made it a point to tell everyone that I saw some rats down here." She laughed. "After that, I knew no one would even think to come to the storage room."

I cringed and suddenly felt a crawling sensation all over my skin. *I really hope she was lying about the rats. . . .*

"The rest was a cinch," she bragged. "I already had my job at the construction site, which gave me access to all the equipment I needed to dig the tunnel to the bank. Just like I did for the other heists. I already had the experience with other companies, and because these construction-type jobs are temporary, the supervisors are usually just happy to find good help. They don't tend to ask a lot of questions."

"But how come no one realized you were stealing equipment?" I asked, glancing over at the drill and auger. Before Penny could reply, I figured out the answer myself. "You were the one recording the inventory when George and I visited you at the construction yard. You changed the records."

"'One drill and auger, out for repairs,'" she quoted proudly. "All I had to do was mark it on a piece of paper."

"Very clever," I admitted.

Penny cocked her head, obviously pleased. "I'm glad you think so, Nancy. I've worked very hard to perfect my operation, and it's so nice to be appreciated." She peered into the passageway and shouted, "Liam! I'm tired of waiting! We are running twenty-five minutes late and counting!" before going back to impatiently staring at her phone.

They're not the only ones running out of time, I thought,

pulling at the belt around my wrists with no success. If I didn't figure out a way to escape soon, I'd find myself in the trunk of a car, headed off to some deserted spot on the River Heights border.

I looked around for something I could use to help, but there were depressingly few items in the room. Any hope I'd had of setting off an alarm or shorting an electrical fuse was gone. And all this thinking was making my head hurt. After the week I'd had, I was kind of surprised that *everything* didn't hurt.

But then my aching head gave me an idea. With Penny distracted, I took the opportunity to scoot myself a little closer to the stairs. Even a few extra feet could make a difference when it came time to run. Once I'd gotten as close as I dared, I took a deep breath and started moaning softly, letting my head loll to the side a little before shaking it back and forth and trying to sit up again.

It was enough to get Penny's attention. She glanced down at me, one eyebrow raised. "What's your problem?" she asked.

I allowed a few seconds to pass before replying. "What do you mean?" I made sure to slur my words slightly.

Penny squinted. "You're acting *weird*."

I looked up at her, my head unsteady, eyes unfocused. "Probably a concussion," I said, still slurring. "I've had them before. Liam hit me pretty hard."

Now Penny actually looked concerned. "How many have you had before?"

I shrugged. "I don't remember. I might have gotten one a few days ago when I got mugged on the street. But, hey, what do you care?" I started to hyperventilate, making my unsteady movements more pronounced.

"Hey, I'm a bank robber, not a *monster*."

"Whatever you have to tell yourself to sleep at night." I groaned. Then, without warning, I rolled my eyes up into my head, made a gurgling sound in my throat, and collapsed.

I'd fallen straight back, which was awkward because my hands were tied behind me, but I had to be in the right position if my plan had any chance of working.

"Ugh," I heard Penny grumble in frustration. "Great, just great. This is the last thing I need tonight. . . ." I sensed her approaching my side to investigate. My eyes were closed, so I waited until I felt Penny's shadow fall over me, and the heat of her breath on my skin before—

I opened my eyes and kicked her right in the stomach.

"Oof!" She stumbled backward onto the floor, gasping for breath.

It wasn't the best kick in the world, but it gave me a few extra seconds to get myself off the floor and bolt up the stairs.

"Liam!" I heard Penny scream from the cellar. *"She's getting away!"*

I reached the training room and made for the front door instead of the back one, even though it was closer. *I'm more likely to find help on the street than the alley.* But I didn't get far. Before I could even cross the room, I crashed full tilt into a large figure and bounced back onto the floor. Thankfully, the mats were soft, and I was actually getting pretty used to falling. I felt a spark of hope. *Someone's here! I'm saved!*

I scrambled to my feet, but when I looked to see the face of my rescuer, my heart dropped back into the pit of my stomach. He was dusting off his hooded jacket—which was ripped at the hem. *The guy in the alley*, I thought, remembering the dark figure getting caught on the wire fence. Then a second person came in from the lobby. Both men wore dark clothing, black caps, and gloves. In the dim light, I could just make out their faces—faces I'd only ever seen in the *River Heights Bugle*. In mug shots.

Max and Ollie Ladrao.

Somehow, instead of the situation getting better, things had just gotten much, much worse.

CHAPTER TWELVE

~

Attack the Back

AS I STOOD IN THE DIMLY LIT ACADEMY, contemplating how I'd become stuck inside a criminal sandwich, I turned to see Penny and Liam emerge from the cellar and zero in on me.

"Get her!" Penny shouted, pointing.

But she and Liam made it only a few steps into the room before noticing Max and Ollie, standing like phantoms in the dark. Liam stopped dead in his tracks. I saw an expression of panic cross Penny's face before she quickly wiped it clean.

"Hello, Max, Ollie," she said, motioning to each

in turn. "So nice of you to drop by. Unfortunately, my associate and I are in a bit of a rush, so we've got to run—"

"I don't think so," Max growled, cracking his knuckles.

"You and your *associate*," Ollie said, "aren't going anywhere until you give us what's ours."

Penny's nostrils flared. "Yours? Hardly. How in the world did you two idiots even find me?"

Ollie smiled. "Oh, we've known you were here for about a month now. Ever since you were foolish enough to put your face in the paper."

"Ugh," Penny groaned. "I knew being in that group picture was a mistake." I wasn't sure what she meant until I remembered the framed article in the lobby. There *had* been a team photo in it, hadn't there?

"You looked different, but I could still recognize you anywhere," Ollie said. "You can change your face all you want, but I still know what you are in *here*." He pointed to his chest.

"And what's that?" Penny asked.

Ollie's lips curled into a sneer. "A *traitor*," he growled.

"We thought that maybe you were planning something and were going to help us out," Max added. "But then we met Kurt—"

Penny snorted. "I knew it. Kurt and his big, dumb mouth—"

"And we knew that you'd ratted us out," Ollie said. "You weren't going to help us—you were the one who put us away in the first place. So we broke out. Turns out, we don't need you, after all."

"Debatable," Penny muttered.

"We followed you, watched you for a few days, coming here and acting like you were the girl next door," Ollie went on. "At first all we wanted to do was scare you. To make you pay for what you did to us. But when I saw the way you were cozying up to this sneaky fool"—he pointed to Liam—"and found those scribbled notes in your locker the night I broke in to start the fire, I realized you were planning another heist. So we figured, what better way to get back the cash that you owe us from that last job than wait until you steal it yourself?"

"Yeah," Max agreed. "Thanks for doing all the work. Now give us what we deserve."

"Oh, I'll give it to you, all right," said Penny, stepping toward the brothers and curling her hands into fists.

"Penny! Hold on," Liam said, grabbing her arm and pulling her back. "If we get into a brawl with these guys and the cops show up, *none* of us are getting out of here with the money. So cool it, okay? I'll get rid of them. You finish cleaning up in the cellar, and then we can get the money and go."

Penny glared at Max and Ollie but stood down. "All right, Ginger," she said. "Have it your way. You might be good for something after all." She gave the brothers one last dirty look before turning to head back through the door to the cellar.

Thankfully, throughout their exchange, no one was really paying attention to me, so I figured it was as good a time as any to get out of there. While Max,

Ollie, and Liam were focused on getting ready to beat one another senseless, I made a beeline for the lobby.

"Oh no, you don't!" Max said, moving to block me. I dodged around him but wasn't quick enough to avoid Ollie grabbing me by the wrist. He pulled me back and wrapped his arm around my neck. I tried to slide out from his grip—but it was no use.

"You're in the wrong place at the wrong time, honey," Ollie muttered in a low, dangerous voice.

No kidding, I thought, struggling in his grip.

Hearing the commotion, Penny came back into the training room and took in the scene. "You all are *really* starting to get on my nerves," she said irritably. "What do you think you're doing, Ollie?"

He shifted, wrapping his hand around my throat where his arm had been. "Give us the money, or I'll start squeezing." I tensed as his fingers dug into my skin.

Penny snorted. "If you think I care what happens to that meddling little—"

I guess I could have waited to hear how she was

going to finish that insult. Brat? Punk? Troublemaker? The world will never know. Instead I decided it was time to turn the tables on these bullies. With all the strength I had left, I lowered myself into a squat and rammed my elbows back between Ollie's legs. He howled and folded over, his hands on his knees. Suddenly everyone was shouting at once.

I stumbled away, scanning the room for my best chance at escape.

"Everyone be quiet!" Penny shouted. The three men all went still and silent; they must've been used to taking orders from her. "Look, Max, Ollie. We might have had our differences in the past," she continued in a soft, soothing voice. "But we have a mutual interest, don't we? So why don't we work together to deal with *her*"—she nodded toward me—"and we can work out some kind of arrangement with the cash once we're safely away from here?"

"Who is she, anyway?" asked Ollie.

"A pain in my neck," Penny replied.

"Look," I said, taking a few cautious steps back.

"You all clearly have a lot to talk about. Why don't I just leave you to it?"

Penny rolled her eyes and turned to the brothers. "Do we have a deal?"

Max and Ollie exchanged a look, then nodded. "Fine," Max said.

"Fine," Ollie agreed. They moved to block the way to the lobby and the locker rooms.

I backed away, catching Liam's eye. "Redheads unite?" I pleaded.

He shook his head and started toward me. "Sorry, Nancy," he said. "Not this time."

"C'mon, c'mon, c'mon," I muttered to myself as the three men closed in. "Think!" But there was nowhere to go. I had played my last card. The game was over.

But just as they were about to reach me, the front door of the academy crashed open and three figures ran into the training room. Bess, George, and a certain young reporter.

"Hey, guys!" Z said, waving excitedly. "Guess what? We called the police!"

I smiled. Looked like the game wasn't over yet. I'd had an ace up my sleeve after all. Or rather, a Z.

"The cops!" Max yelled.

"Liam, grab the gym bag with the cash, quick!" Penny commanded. "We've got to get out of here, now!"

Liam nodded and ran down into the cellar, emerging seconds later with the black gym bag. "But what about the rest of the money?" he asked, panting. "There's only a few thousand in here!"

"You want your money or your freedom?" she demanded. "We're out of time! There'll always be more banks to rob!"

While they were bickering, Bess, George, and Z ran up to me. "Nancy!" said Bess. "Are you okay?"

"I'm fine, but they're going to get away!"

"Go, go, go!" Penny was shouting, waving Liam toward the back door. Max and Ollie followed on his heels, rushing to get away.

"I'm going!" Liam said, and slammed his hand against the crash bar. It swung open, but instead of revealing the dark alley that ran behind the academy, something else was waiting there. Something that made me feel better than I had all week.

Nearly the entire Iron Dragon team—Carly, Nate, Jake, Jeremy, Tim, Ernesto, and a few others—stood in the doorway, with Coach Ethan right at the front.

Liam stumbled back into the Ladrao brothers behind him. "E-Ethan . . . ," he stammered.

Coach Ethan crossed his arms over his chest and slowly shook his head. "I'm disappointed in you, Liam. Not only did you betray the entire team, but you didn't even see this coming. Did you forget the first rule of Jiu-Jitsu?"

Liam's face went pale. "Attack the back."

Ethan turned to his team. "Get this trash out of my school," he said softly.

The Iron Dragons poured into the room, circling Liam, Max, and Ollie like a pack of wolves. Max tried to make a run for the lobby, but just as he was passing, Bess dived, grabbing him around the waist and executing a perfect takedown.

"Ahhh!" Max yelled as he fell flat on his face, hitting the mats with a crash.

Bess leaped onto his back as soon as he was down, hanging on for dear life as he bucked like a wild horse, trying to shake her off. Ernesto jogged over and bent close.

"May I step in, young lady?" he asked politely.

Bess, her face glistening with sweat, yet somehow radiating pure joy, looked up at him and grinned. "Why sure, Tall, Dark, and Handsome. Be my guest!" She nimbly hopped off Max's back, and an instant later Ernesto had hopped on like they were taking turns on a carnival ride. Within moments, Ernesto had wrapped himself around Max like a snake and was pulling him into a backbreaking position.

"Now, are you going to give us any more trouble?" Ernesto asked, like he was talking to a naughty child.

"No! No!" Max choked out, pulling helplessly on Ernesto's arm. "No more trouble!"

"Good boy," Ernesto said, releasing his grip. Max

lay on his back, gasping for air. Ernesto motioned to Bess and George. "Will one of you help me tie him up?"

"Here!" I said, turning away from them. "Untie me and use the belt for him instead."

While George released me from my bonds, Bess knelt next to Ernesto and said, "That move was amazing. What's it called?"

"A bow and arrow choke," Ernesto replied. "Elegant, isn't it?"

"When this is all over, can you teach me?" asked Bess.

"Of course, *tigresa*," Ernesto said with a wink. "You'll be a warrior in no time."

My hands finally free, I rubbed my wrists and surveyed the room. Ollie and Liam were on their knees, their hands raised in surrender, with at least three grapplers around each of them. I could hear the sound of sirens approaching.

But where was Penny?

"Coach Ethan!" I called out, dashing across the room to his side.

"Nancy Drew," he said, smiling when he saw me. "Looks like we got here just in time, huh?"

"Yes," I said quickly, "but I don't see Penny anywhere."

Coach Ethan scanned the room. "Shoot, she must have slipped out while we were focused on the others—Nancy, wait!"

But I had already taken off out the back door to the alley. It was just wide enough to accommodate Penny's small white sedan, which was parked right near the door. She was there, bending to throw the gym bag full of cash into the back seat. The car was already running, its headlights piercing the darkness. I moved in front of the sedan, blocking her passage back onto the street.

"It's over, Penny," I said.

She startled, banging her head against the roof of the car. She emerged a moment later, rubbing the tender spot and scowling. "You know, Nancy," she said, slamming the back door shut, "I can't decide if you're really smart, or just really lucky."

"Eh, it's probably a little of both," I replied. "But honestly, luck can only get you so far."

"Oh, I don't know," Penny said, chuckling without humor. "I used to have a nickname in the crime circles, back when I first started pulling jobs—Lucky Penny. Never got caught, not once. And I'm not about to let a silly little nothing like you break my streak."

"I think you underestimate the lengths I'll go in order to close a case," I said. "I'm a little bit obsessed. Ask anyone. So"— I lowered myself into a defensive crouch—"if you want to get out of here, you'll have to go through me first."

Penny laughed, but then stopped abruptly when she realized how serious I was. "Don't tempt me, Nancy," she said, her voice a warning.

I narrowed my eyes. "Consider yourself tempted."

"Have it your way," Penny growled. With a shout, she came tearing toward me, her fist raised to deliver a knockout punch. I tensed—I was talking a big game, but I wasn't sure if my bruised and battered body could take another hit.

Time seemed to slow as she stepped into the brightness of the headlights, and I watched as her outstretched arm moved within my reach.

Get your grips, a voice in my mind said.

All I wanted to do was to run away, to cover my face and hide. After all, I was an amateur detective, not a professional fighter. But the voice only got louder.

You have to believe.

And suddenly I imagined myself back in class, on the mats with Liam, repeating that specific twisting movement over and over. I remembered how it felt, how my body moved.

Don't think.

Penny's fist was inches from my face now.

Just do it.

I reached out, grabbed Penny's wrist, and then twisted around until my back was to her. Using her forward momentum, I loaded her body up onto my back and—almost effortlessly—threw her over my shoulder and onto the cold, hard ground.

Penny lay on her back, staring up at the sky. "You *threw* me!" she said in disbelief.

"Eyyyyyy!" Coach Ethan called, coming outside.

"Not too bad for a white belt, Nancy!"

A few other faces, including Bess's and George's, peeped out the back door. "The police are here," George reported. "They're taking Max, Ollie, and Liam into custody."

Penny's eyes closed in defeat. I was pretty sure her days of bank robbing and identity hopping were finished. "Looks like your luck finally ran out," I said to her.

A moment later a police officer pushed through the crowd and out into the alley. The bearded young man sighed when he saw me. "If this is your idea of staying out of trouble, Miss Drew," he said, "I think you might need to reevaluate your definition of 'trouble.'"

"Officer Nadeem," I said with a small smile. "Fancy meeting you here."

He surveyed the scene. "It's nice of you to do so much of the work for me, but how about I take over from here?"

I nodded, relieved, and allowed Coach Ethan and the others to lead me back inside while Officer

Nadeem read Penny her rights and put her in handcuffs. My shoulders were aching, my head throbbed, and I desperately needed some water. And maybe a pizza. A large pizza. All for me.

Back inside, the other police officers were leading Max, Ollie, and Liam out to their squad cars. Red and blue lights were flashing through the picture window and making the whole academy look like a disco party. The Iron Dragon team gave me fist bumps as I passed by. At the back of the group was Z.

"Hey, Nancy!" he said cheerfully, as if stopping bank robberies was something he did every day. "Good to see you again! You left your purse back at the *Bugle*." He handed it to me.

I took it from him gratefully. "Thanks," I said. "But how did you know to come here?"

"Well," he said, rubbing the back of his head, "I tried to text and call you about your purse after you rushed out, and when you didn't pick up, I got worried and called Bess. We'd exchanged numbers when she came back to train at Lockdown, so she knew who

I was." He chuckled. "She made me promise to save her number under 'Anastasia Blackstone.' Anyway, as soon as I told her where you had gone, she knew you'd need backup. So she said she'd contact everyone and get them over here right away."

"Wait, so Bess and George never got a text from me?"

The cousins in question walked up, catching the end of our conversation. They both shook their heads. "A text? No," Bess said. "I did think it was a little strange that I didn't hear from you all day, but sometimes you get so wrapped up in a case. I tried texting you earlier to ask for an update and didn't hear back— but I honestly didn't think too much of it until I got the call from Z."

"Wow," I said, putting a hand to my chest. I turned to the young reporter and grabbed him by the shoulders. "I don't know what to say, Z. If you hadn't gotten in touch with my friends, I'd probably be locked in a trunk, crammed in with a bunch of stolen cash right now. Or worse. I owe you, big-time."

Z blushed and looked down at the floor. "Well,

thanks, Nancy. I was just doing what I thought was right."

"So," I said, smiling. "I think I have an idea that might just get you that front-page story."

Z's eyes lit up. "You'll give me an exclusive?"

"Of course! It's the least I can do!"

"Omigosh," Z said, digging into his bag for a notebook and pen. "This could be huge for me, Nancy. *Huge!* Let me start by interviewing some of the others here for background, and maybe I can call you later for the full scoop, if you're up for it?"

"Absolutely."

While Z went to talk to Coach Ethan and a few of the other members of the team, Officer Nadeem joined Bess, George, and me. His thick brows were furrowed in concern. "Nancy, we have a problem."

"What's wrong?"

"We found the gym bag full of cash in the car, but that only accounts for a few thousand dollars at most. I got in touch with the bank manager, and according to him, there was close to a million dollars in that vault. But my officers say that the bags in there are full of nothing but sand. So where's the rest of the money? Penny and Liam aren't talking. Did you happen to overhear them saying where they might have stashed it?"

I thought back on everything that had happened over the past couple of hours. "They were really vague about it," I said. "Penny did mention that moving the money was a 'two-man job,' though. So, something bulky or heavy?"

Bess shook her head. "Where could you possibly hide almost a million dollars in cash in this place?" she wondered aloud.

I slowly walked around the room, my shoes crunching on the still-sandy floor. My eyes passed over the mats, the exercise equipment, some shelves and chairs, the punching bags—

Wait a second.

"George," I called. "Do you still keep a Swiss Army knife in your purse?"

She rummaged around in her bag for a minute

before pulling out a small red pocketknife. "Here you go," she said, handing it over. "Why? What do you need it for?"

"I have a hunch," I replied. I walked down the line of punching bags, pushing each one with my hand. The first three were extremely heavy and barely moved. But the fourth one swung much more easily when I gave it a shove. I turned to Coach Ethan, who was watching me, curious. "If I'm wrong," I told him, "I promise I'll fix it." And with that, I flicked open one of the blades, stabbed it into the punching bag, and ripped a long tear in the thick fabric.

Usually, punching bags are filled with sand, but that wasn't what spilled out of the opening.

"Oh my goodness," Bess exclaimed. "The money!"

Sure enough, bundles of hundred-dollar bills poured out onto the floor, and it was clear that there was much more where that came from.

Officer Nadeem walked over and stood in front of the gutted punching bag, hands on hips. "How did you know?" he asked me.

"It was something Jeremy said yesterday when George and I saw him training before class. Something about one of the bags not being as heavy as usual. 'Either I'm getting stronger, or this bag is getting lighter,' he said. It was just an offhand comment, but remembering just now, it made me think that a punching bag would be a perfect place to store a bunch of cash. But Penny would've had to empty it out a little at a time. She must've opened up a seam and removed the sand slowly so the students using the bag wouldn't really notice. That's why there's been so much sand all over the floor. Then, when she was ready, she could empty out the rest of the sand to fill up the bags in the vault, making them still look full, and stuff all the money inside the punching bag. Tonight, all she and Liam would have needed to do was hoist the bag off its hook and drop the whole thing in the back seat of their car. Plus, if anyone had stopped them on the road to search the car, they wouldn't think to look inside a punching bag. It was the perfect hiding place—the perfect crime."

"It certainly would have been, if it weren't for you,"

Officer Nadeem said, patting me on the back. "Good work, Nancy."

"It actually took me quite a few wrong turns to get there, but . . ." I suddenly felt really dizzy. I almost lost my balance, but luckily, Officer Nadeem caught me and pulled me over to one of the folding chairs at the side of the mats. Sagging into the seat, I murmured my thanks and tried to breathe deeply.

"Are you hurt?" he asked. I never really liked getting that kind of attention, and a crowd was starting to form around us, making me feel even more silly.

"I'm fine, really," I said, squeezing my eyes closed to stop the room from spinning. "I mean, I got a pretty good wallop to the back of my head earlier. For maybe the third time this week. But I swear, give me a Coke and a few slices of pizza and I'll be good to go."

Carly, dressed in the same hooded sweatshirt she'd been wearing when we'd first met out on the street, rushed over, pushing through to my side. "Don't be ridiculous, Nancy," she said. "You need to be checked out. Let me take a look—I've had some paramedic training." She turned to the group. "Can we get Nancy a Gatorade or something?"

While Ryan rushed to grab a drink from the lobby, Carly turned to me and started asking some questions and testing my vision. Ryan handed me a yellow Gatorade, and I drank half of it in one gulp. The sugar almost instantly made me feel more alert, and after a few minutes, I felt like I finally had gotten off the merry-go-round. "I think it's just a mild concussion," Carly said, squatting in front of me. "But you should still go to the hospital to get checked out."

I grimaced. "That's what I figured. Thanks, Carly."

"Me?" Carly shook her head, eyes wide. "Thank *you*, Nancy, for saving our academy. I'm just so relieved this whole thing wasn't about my tournament. Now I can really focus on the competing."

I sat straight up, almost spilling the rest of the Gatorade all over myself. "The tournament!" I exclaimed. "That's tomorrow, isn't it?"

"It sure is," Coach Ethan said. "The police are almost done here, so the competitors should get home to bed. You guys need to rest up for the big day."

"Are you going to come watch?" Carly asked me.

"Your fights?" I replied. "Do you want me to?"

"Are you kidding?" she said, laughing. "You and your friends are part of the team now. Of course I want you to be there!"

I smiled. "Well then, I wouldn't miss it for the world!"

CHAPTER THIRTEEN

~

Winning and Learning

"OH WOW, THIS IS SO EXCITING!" BESS SAID as we walked into the River Heights Sports Complex the next morning. I'd only ever been in the building to watch one of my friends play field hockey, so I had no idea what awaited us inside.

"Um, Bess? Are you wearing a Jiu-Jitsu T-shirt?" George asked.

I squinted at Bess's black tee, which read EAT. SLEEP. TRAIN JIU-JITSU in big block letters. "Seriously?" I asked. "It's been literally less than a week."

Bess shrugged. "What? Ernesto gave it to me.

And he's already given me a Jiu-Jitsu nickname, too! Tigresa—it's Brazilian for 'lady tiger.' You know, because I'm *fierce*." She beamed.

George and I exchanged a look. "She's obsessed," George muttered out of the corner of her mouth.

"I know the case is closed," Bess went on, "but you guys are going to keep training, right?"

George sucked her teeth. "I don't know," she said. "My schedule is pretty full. . . . And as much as I love having strangers sweat into my eyeballs, it wasn't *exactly* my idea of a good time."

"Weak," Bess said, rolling her eyes. "How about you, Nancy? I know you enjoyed it. Didn't Coach Ethan promise to teach you for free if you solved the case? *And* your dad wanted you to learn self-defense. Think of your future as a detective! Think of all those bad guys you'll be able to take down!"

Bess was giving me her patented doe-eyed stare, which, coupled with her heart-shaped face and blue eyes, was difficult to resist at the best of times. "Let me think about it," I managed. I was still nursing a mild concussion and enough bruises to make me look like a jaguar, so the thought of being back on the mats again wasn't particularly appealing. It had been a tough and exhausting case, and I needed a break.

The sports complex was crowded and alive with noise and excitement. A sea of mats was laid out in the middle of the arena behind waist-high plastic barriers. On each square, there were fights already in progress. Referees watched intently, coaches shouted commands, and fans stood behind the barriers, cheering the competitors on. Around the edges of the room, more than a hundred other grapplers dressed in Jiu-Jitsu gis of all different colors, each one patched with their team's logo, awaited their chance to fight.

I scanned the room, searching for our friends, and finally spotted fighters with the roaring silver dragon logo on the other side of the room. "They're over there!" I called out to Bess and George before we made our way over.

"Nancy Drew," Coach Ethan said, slapping me on the back. "So, you coming to class on Monday?"

I blinked. "I mean, I don't know," I said. "I *was* just kidnapped by bank robbers. . . ."

"Excuses, excuses," he said, shaking his head. "Anyway, you made it just in time! Carly's division is about to start. She's already waiting down in the bullpen."

"How many fights does she need to win?" George asked.

"Four to medal, five for gold," Coach Ethan replied. "I've got to get down there to coach. See you on the other side, champ!" He smiled and gave me a thumbs-up before jogging away.

I watched him go, shaking my head. "What kind of mind game is he playing, anyway?"

"I don't know, but it's working, isn't it?" Bess said wryly.

I crossed my arms. "Maybe," I muttered.

A few minutes later, after saying hello to the rest of the team, we went down to the mat where Carly was scheduled to fight. On the way, I saw "Master" Brock from Lockdown walk by with his team, including

Lucy Hayes. Brock didn't have anything to do with the crime at Iron Dragon, it was true, but there was still no excuse for the way he'd treated Carly. The hulking coach gazed around the arena like he owned the place. Lucy looked nervous.

Brock stopped when he caught sight of me and Bess and waved. "Well, hello, ladies," he said, putting on his most winning smile. "Nice to see you again, Ana. Come to watch the best and brightest go for gold, eh? That's good. So, when can I get you both in the office to sign up for full memberships? I do private lessons as well, you know. Extra charge, but very worth it. You'll get your blue belts in no time."

Bess and I exchanged glances. "Sorry, Mr. Vaughn," I said. "But we've already chosen a team." I nodded toward the Iron Dragons, who were all gathered to watch Carly's first fight.

Brock followed my gaze, and when he saw who I was referring to, his face turned as red as a cherry. Lucy was standing next to him, listening. Her eyes widened as she caught sight of her former friend.

"You're making a big mistake," Brock said, trying with difficulty to keep that smile pasted on. "Iron Dragon is no place for you. It will take you *years* to be promoted over there, do you understand? You'll get steamrollered by those guys. If you come to Lockdown, you'll move up in the ranks like everyone else. Isn't that what you want?"

"Thanks, but no thanks," I replied. "If there's one thing I've learned about Jiu-Jitsu over this past week, it's that honor isn't given, it's earned."

Brock scowled. "Fine," he said, all trace of his charm gone. "Have it your way. But we'll see whose champion will be left standing at the top of that podium." He stomped away, but Lucy didn't budge. She stood staring at us, seemingly lost in thought. A moment later Brock turned back and called out to her. "Let's go, Lucy! Your first match is in five minutes!"

Tearing her eyes away from us, Lucy turned to follow her coach to the warm-up area.

The girls and I made our way through the crowd. Coach Ethan was already sitting on a chair beside the mat, waiting for the match to begin. Carly's first opponent—a very tall girl with curly black hair and bronze skin—looked way bigger than her, even though they were in the same division. "Oh man," I said to Tim, who'd squeezed in next to me. "That girl is huge!"

He chuckled. "She might *look* bigger. But Carly's going to wipe the floor with her anyway. Just watch."

Tim's right, I thought as I studied Carly's face. *She doesn't look worried at all!*

Carly and the other girl bumped fists, and the referee shouted, *"Combate!"* I bit my lip as the two girls circled each other like a pair of lions. After some feints, the other girl lunged for Carly's collar. But she was ready for it. Before her opponent's hand could connect, Carly dove down and tackled the girl with an elegant takedown. The girl toppled like a felled tree, and Carly was on top of her in an instant, locking her forearm over the girl's neck. Before I could even understand what was happening, the girl tapped the mat, and the match was over.

The whole thing took about thirty seconds.

The team around me was going crazy. "CARLYYYYYY!" they roared as one. Carly stood up and casually adjusted her gi top before walking over to the referee. The tall girl, who looked a bit like she'd been struck by lightning, did the same. The referee grabbed both their wrists and waited a moment before raising Carly's arm as the winner.

Carly came over and exchanged a few words with Coach Ethan before she noticed us. "Nancy!" she said, her serious face lighting up with a smile. "You made it!"

"Darn right I did!" I said, giving her a fist bump. "I'm so excited to see you in action!"

She took a long drink from her water bottle. "Well, that was the easy one, unfortunately," she said, wiping the perspiration from her face. "That girl was a brand-new purple belt, so I was pretty sure I could win the match. The other four girls won't be as easy to beat."

I put my hand on Carly's shoulder. "You've got this."

"I'll do my best," she said, then turned back to the mat for her next fight.

As Carly predicted, the next few matchups were nail-biters. In one of them, she was down by points and only ended up getting the submission in the last ten seconds. In the semifinal, the points were tied up until the very end, and Carly was given the judge's decision, winning that match too. Everyone on the team breathed a sigh of relief. She'd made it to the finals!

I thought Carly was smiling as she walked off the mat after the semifinal, but as she got closer, I saw that she was actually grimacing with pain.

Oh no!

Coach Ethan and the rest of the team gathered around her. "What happened?" the coach asked, his brows furrowed in concern.

"It's my hand," Carly said, wincing as she lifted it to show him. "My fingers got jammed during the match, and they're starting to swell up. I can't bend them."

Coach Ethan called the medic over, and after a quick examination, she announced that though the fingers weren't broken, they were pretty badly sprained. "I would consider quitting while you're ahead, young lady," the medic said as she taped Carly's fingers together. Once the medic had gone, Carly turned back to Coach Ethan.

"I can't forfeit now," she said, still a little breathless with the pain. "Did you see who I'm fighting in the finals?"

Coach Ethan nodded grimly. "I know."

"Lucy Hayes," I muttered.

Tim nodded. "Carly's archenemy."

The tension and excitement in the room were palpable. "Omigosh, what I wouldn't give for some popcorn right now!" George said, her palms pressed against her cheeks.

The referee motioned to get Carly's attention. "Miss Griffith, the final match will start in a few minutes. Are you ready?"

"I'll be there in a minute," she said. The referee nodded and walked away. Carly started to pace behind the barrier. "I don't know, I don't know," she mumbled. She turned to Coach Ethan. "Coach, what do I do?"

Coach Ethan spoke softly, so I had to lean in to hear

the words. "Listen," he said to her. "You don't need to prove anything to Lucy, or me, or anyone else—do you understand? If you want to do this, do it for yourself."

Carly took a deep breath and closed her eyes, tilting her face upward. She stood there silent as everyone looked on, waiting. Finally she opened her eyes; her expression was calm but determined as she walked over to speak to the referee.

By this point, Lucy had arrived. She was standing on the other side of the mat with Brock Vaughn. They were both staring intently at Carly.

I held my breath. What had she decided to do?

A moment later the referee nodded and walked to the center of the mat. He faced the crowd and called the two competitors in. The Iron Dragon and Lockdown teams cheered. The match was on!

"This is for the gold," I overheard Brock say to Lucy. "Go hard right off the bat. You see her hand? She's hurt, and there's no rule against taking advantage of that. Take her down, Hayes."

Bess and George heard it too. "Hey!" Bess said,

squaring her shoulders. "That's not fair! We should say something—"

I put my hand on her arm. "No, Bess, we can't. It's like Brock said: there's no rule against Lucy changing her strategy because of Carly's injury. Carly agreed to the fight, and everything that comes with it. We have to trust that she's got it under control."

Bess sighed. "Yeah, I guess you're right."

I sounded calm and confident. On the inside, though, I felt anything but.

The crowd was riveted as Carly and Lucy faced each other, slapped hands, and bumped fists. The referee chopped his arm down between them and yelled, *"Combate!"* and the fight began.

Following Brock's instructions, Lucy wasted no time at all. She immediately stepped in and got her grips on Carly's collar and sleeve. Carly tried to break them, but it wasn't easy with only one hand. Lucy snapped her down and waited for Carly to stand up straight again before she dove in low, grabbing at Carly's legs in an attempt to take her to the ground. Working on instinct, Carly put her hands out to slap the mat and break her fall, but in doing so, she slammed her injured fingers onto the ground. A gasp of pain escaped her lips and Lucy hunkered down for the kill, setting up a choke that would end the match.

All around me, the Iron Dragon team's spirits started to sink.

"I don't know much about Jiu-Jitsu," George whispered to me, "but this is bad, right? This looks bad."

Bess nodded. "She's down two points for the takedown. She's in a tough spot, but it's not over yet. . . ."

Coach Ethan was leaning so far forward in his chair, it looked like he was going to fall out of it. "Get out of there, Carly," he was shouting. "Don't let her get that elbow in. You know what to do! Push, Carly—*PUSH!*"

I'm not sure what came over me. I guess I was just caught up in the moment. After all, I knew what it was like to feel as if there was no hope left.

But I also knew that those were the moments when you needed your friends the most.

Leaning over the plastic barrier, I shouted, "You can do it, Carly!"

Bess looked at me, surprised and delighted, then yelled, "Yeah, Carly! You're unstoppable!"

The rest of the team joined in, shouting Carly's name and cheering her on. I saw something change in Carly's face, hearing all those voices, like she was digging deep to find the last ounce of strength she had left.

A moment later, she scooted to the side—changing her angle—and without even using her injured hand, bridged her hips up and flipped Lucy over. Lucy was so surprised to find her opponent on top of her, she didn't even have a chance to defend the armbar before Carly locked it on. Lucy tapped the mat furiously, and just like that, it was over.

The entire crowd around me erupted in cheers. Carly had done it! She'd won gold!

With her injured hand tucked into her gi, she let the referee lift her other arm in victory.

She was walking back to us, a huge smile on her

face, when Lucy stopped her a few feet from the barrier where we were all waiting. I winced, worried that she would say something mean and ruin the moment.

"Hey, Carly," Lucy said nervously. "That was a great fight. Congratulations."

Carly's eyebrows went up. "Oh . . . thanks, Lucy. You too."

Lucy shook her head. "Nah, I totally botched that match."

Carly put a hand on Lucy's shoulder. "Hey, don't be so hard on yourself. You know what they say: you either win or you learn."

Lucy looked up at Carly's kind face and seemed to make a decision. "So, um, listen," she said. "I know I messed up back at Lockdown, and I'm really sorry. You were right about Brock. You were right about *every-thing*." Her face creased with emotion. "The truth is, I miss training with you. These past few months, I realized that the only reason I really liked Lockdown was because you were there. It's just not the same now that you're gone."

Carly's eyes softened. "Lucy, I miss you, too. You were the best training partner I've ever had. You're amazing." She grabbed Lucy's hand and squeezed it. "Why don't you come train at Iron Dragon with me?"

"Really?" asked Lucy. "You think your coach would be okay with that?"

"He welcomed me in when I needed a new team," Carly said. "I'm pretty sure he'd do the same for you. Just go and ask him."

Lucy shook her head in disbelief. "I don't understand," she said. "Even after everything that's happened? You'd still want me there?"

Carly grinned, mischief in her eyes. "How about this: whatever we've got left to work out, we can work it out on the mats. Deal?"

Lucy chuckled, her blue eyes sparkling. "Deal."

A few minutes later the whole Iron Dragon team was gathered in front of the podium to watch Carly receive her medal. Lucy stood next to her in the second-place position, looking happier than I'd ever seen her. Brock stood at the edge of the crowd. He looked furious, but no one paid him much attention.

After the medal was placed around Carly's neck and everyone snapped pictures on their phones, I heard a murmur of excitement pass through the crowd. "What is it?" I asked Coach Ethan. "What's going on?"

He smiled. "Master Julian is here."

"Master Julian?" Bess asked. "Who's that?"

"He's the owner, the man who started Iron Dragon," Coach Ethan replied. "The one who taught me Jiu-Jitsu and gave me my black belt."

"Ooh," Bess said, clearly impressed. "He gave *you* your black belt?"

"Mm-hmm," Coach Ethan said with a chuckle. "And he'll never let me forget it."

I craned my neck to see a serious-looking man in jeans and a black T-shirt walking toward the podium with a small bag slung over his shoulder. His black hair was cropped close to his head, and he wore silver wire-rimmed glasses. I recognized him as the man in the team photo on the wall back at the academy. Although he was a full head shorter than Brock Vaughn, he seemed to radiate an energy that made everyone in the crowd turn to watch what he was going to do next.

Carly saw him coming, and all the color drained from her face.

He reached the podium and looked up at her. "Carly," he said in a quiet voice that nonetheless reached every ear in the room. "You did well today. Congratulations." He reached into the bag and pulled out a brown belt. "Keep working hard, and one day you'll have a black belt of your own." For the second time in an hour, every member on the Iron Dragon team lost their minds. Master Julian untied the purple belt from her waist, slung it around her neck, and replaced it with the brown one. Once he'd shaken her hand and stepped back, all her friends ran up onto the podium and took turns hugging her and taking selfies.

I was so busy enjoying the show, I didn't even realize Master Julian was there until he was standing right in front of me.

"Hello," he said.

"Oh!" I exclaimed, a little startled. "Um, hello!"

"Nancy Drew, is it?" Master Julian said. "I'm Julian Kim, founder and owner of Iron Dragon MMA. I've heard quite a lot about you. Something about stopping a bank robbery at the academy last night and rooting out a traitor from our midst."

I blushed. "You make it sound so dramatic."

He raised one eyebrow. "When several criminals, close to a million dollars, and the River Heights Police Department are involved, I would say 'dramatic' is a fair assessment."

"That's true," I admitted.

"I wanted to personally thank you for everything you've done. I hope you'll take Coach Ethan up on his offer and continue to train with us."

I looked away. "Well, my friend Bess is definitely going to keep at it, but I'm just not sure I'm the right kind of person for Jiu-Jitsu."

Master Julian didn't blink. He just regarded me, saying nothing. I felt like he was looking straight into my soul, and I felt a little nervous to know what he'd find there. "You're wrong," he finally said. "And besides, there's no such thing as 'the right kind of person for Jiu-Jitsu.' If you want to learn, that's all you need. So, what do you say?"

I thought for a moment, casting my mind back to where this whole case started: that night with Chef Kathy at the soup kitchen. "How about this," I said. "The community around Iron Dragon needs all the help it can get right now. Do you think you guys could do some free lessons for kids in the neighborhood? Maybe pitch in on some of the community projects going on? People like you and your team could really help us make changes for the better. You guys are heroes, and River Heights needs heroes right now. If you do me that favor, you can have your students throw me around as much as they want."

Master Julian gave a little smile. "You drive a hard bargain, Miss Drew. But I like the way you think. It's a deal." He nodded crisply, then walked away.

I watched him go, my heart feeling very full. I may

have been sore beyond belief, but that moment made it all worthwhile.

Bess and George returned from their hugs and selfies, looking exhilarated. "You know, Bess," George said, "this combat sports thing may not be for me, but it's pretty cool, and I'm glad it makes you happy."

Bess grinned. "Aw, thanks, cuz. So does that mean I can practice my moves on you?"

George laughed. "If you pay me in snacks, I'll consider it."

Bess shoved her cousin playfully before turning to me. "What about you, Nancy? Will you 'roll' with me sometime?"

I grinned. "Sure, Bess. Why not? But right now, all I want is a couch and a pizza. What do you ladies think?"

Bess slapped my hand and gave me a fist bump. "You're on!"

Dear Diary,

WOW—WHAT A BUSY FEW WEEKS! SINCE Penny and Liam were arrested, the Iron Dragon team has been going above and beyond to help out in the community. Coach Ethan and some of the upper belts started teaching about a dozen kids from the neighborhood, and Libby organized a fundraiser at the local pizza shop to buy them all brand-new gear. Some of the other team members started joining me at the soup kitchen every week too—Kathy couldn't be happier to have all those extra hands at mealtime! It's awesome to see these athletes not only fighting on the mat, but also fighting for a better future for our city.

Bess has been training three times a week and loves it more and more each day. I've gone with her to class a few times, and I have to admit, Jiu-Jitsu really is a lot of fun! She's already planning on doing her first competition in a few months. She says she's totally freaked out, but she wants to do it anyway. I'm so happy for her— facing down bad guys is great, but facing your fears? Now that's something that really deserves a medal.